THE GRAND OLE OPRY MURDERS

THE GRAND OLE OPRY MURDERS

MARVIN KAYE

NEW YORK

SATURDAY REVIEW PRESS/E. P. DUTTON & CO., INC.

Published simultaneously in Canada by Clarke, Irwin & Company
Limited, Toronto and Vancouver

To Rose and Lou Bransdorf
with love and thanks
beyond my spoken power to express

ACKNOWLEDGMENTS

Though they are in no way to be considered as endorsing, sanctioning, approving or acquiescing to what follows, thanks are due, nonetheless, to the Country Music Association, Opryland U.S.A., the Nashville Chamber of Commerce, the Country Music Hall of Fame and Museum, and miscellaneous personnel of the Grand Ole Opry and NBC–TV for their valuable technical assistance and for making materials available to the author without which the book could not have been written.

Thanks to Terry Ziegler and the editorial department of GRIT Publishing Co., Williamsport, Pennsylvania, for permission to reprint the article on Camotillo from the June 27, 1965 (page twelve) issue of that venerable newspaper.

I am especially indebted to Dr. Irwin J. Cohen and also Frank Garner, David Goldenberg and Alan Warren for supplying information on toxicity and for their help in attempting to track down further information concerning Camotillo.

THE GRAND OLE OPRY MURDERS

1

She was rehearsing at the Grand Ole Opry in Nashville when she swallowed the poison. I was there. It was the third time I had heard her sing.

The first occasion was in Hilary Quayle's office, and I didn't want to listen in the worst way. "Look," I told my employer, "I don't like one-night stands, I'm not crazy about traveling through the South, and country-western music makes me sick! The most recent popular songwriter I can stomach is John Dowland, and he's been dead a couple of hundred years."

She pretended to ignore me. But it didn't take, mostly because I could see a little humorous uptilt creasing the corner of her mouth, Hilary's version of a chuckle. "This," she explained while positioning the tonearm on the edge of the demo disc, "is Amanda's latest hit."

"All right," I objected, swiveling in my chair so I could prop an elbow on the desktop, "if I *have* to listen, I will, but you're not going to make me change my mind."

The music began. It was a clean sound without any strings

or electronic showiness, "basic Nashville," as I've since heard it called.

Hilary sat down next to the phonograph in a spot where she could study my reaction without having to stare straight into my eyes. I swore to myself that, no matter what I thought, I would display no trace of enthusiasm. . . .

But then I heard Amanda Boulder sing. Though her voice was basically untrained, lacking professional technique in its placement, the phrasing was impeccable and the timbre so warm and eloquent that I almost considered writing her a love letter, sight unseen. It was a sorrowful lyric, and the vocalist made the most of it, every now and then letting a poignant catch in her voice add to the keening effect.

I have seen your eyes and know that they are yearning,
I have fled them down the years, but all in vain,
And the sorrow in my heart is always burning
For I'll never call you sweetheart again.
[Chorus] No, I'll never call you sweetheart again.
    Oh, I'll never call you sweetheart again.
    You're my dearest love, my angel, you're my darling,
    But I'll never call you sweetheart again.
I have friends who talk of luxury and money
And a fame that I am told will never pall
But I'll never reach that land of milk and honey
And instead I shed these bitter tears of gall.
    Oh, I'll never call you sweetheart again . . .
Well, I cry each time I dream I hear you singing,
Though the pain I feel is nothing like your pain.
Yet no other love will come to ease the stinging
And I'll never call you sweetheart again.
    No, I'll never call you sweetheart again . . .

When it was over, we sat for a moment listening to the needle scratch against the inner groove. Then Hilary got up and shut off the machine. She turned to me and raised an eyebrow, inviting comment.

I shrugged. "How does a person go about shedding gall? Must be kind of messy, bile leaking all over the . . ."

"Don't waste your wit," Hilary snapped. "You can't spare any." She gestured impatiently. "Well? Do you like her?"

I turned my chair so I could face her. "What the hell do you expect me to say? I don't have to tell you what you can hear for yourself. She's great—but she's not a country-western singer."

"And why not?"

"Because she's too good."

"*Oh, my God!*" she murmured, closing her eyes in exasperation. I could practically hear the sarcastic subtext, but she stifled it. Returning to her desk, Hilary rooted through some papers, extracted a stapled cluster of mimeographed sheets and shoved it in my direction. I glanced at it and saw it was a press release, "It Hain't Called Hillbilly No Mo'," issued by the Associated Fan Society of Country Music.

> Nashville stands at the crossroads of the Old South and the American West and the musical heritages of many peoples converged to make it truly Music City, U.S.A. The lonely nights of a cowboy crooning on the trail, the country fiddlin at a Saturday Night Hoedown, the rich humming of the plantation darky, and the birth of the blues in New Orleans all had their parts in the musical melting pot that is Nashville, that has made country music climb to the very nadir of American popular music charts. . . .

I slammed it down on my desk. "Goddamnit, Hilary, you can fire me if you want to, but I'm not going to read this garbage! Look at this, for Chrissake—'*nadir!*' You'd think they'd never heard of a dic—"

I stopped, suddenly feeling ridiculous. Hilary knows lousy

PR writing always makes me mouth off; I looked at her and saw she had a hand over part of her face, but I could tell she was laughing, though the sound was practically inaudible. It was a rare mood for Hilary. In other circumstances, I might have enjoyed it, but now I could see her eyes, sky blue, crinkling merrily at the corners, and I wondered what they might look like with black circles around them.

"I'm sorry, Gene," she said at last, still smiling, "I didn't mean to make fun, but you *are* so predictable."

"And I suppose you're not?" I asked. "If you ever run out of men to take apart, you could always change hobbies and geld stallions."

Once, she slapped me for something like that, and I thought she might repeat the performance, but all she did was stare at me coldly. I wondered for the fiftieth time since Hilary hired me as her secretary months ago why the two of us could never make human contact without squaring off like boxers.

After a moment, she spoke. "Harriet Marker over at the Thomas agency gave my name to the Boulder Clan. Their manager just fired their PR agent and they're interested in giving us the account. You're going to go check them out. Period."

"Now you listen to me," I replied, walking over to her desk and glowering down at her. "I don't know enough about country music to talk meaningfully to the prospective client. That's the first point. Second: I hate 'the road'; it's a lousy way of life and a rotten institution. The food is greasy down there, the constant driving jangles my nerves, and the water in some of those states turns my stomach and gives me dizzy spells. I don't want to go, you can't make me go, and I *won't* go! What do you say to that?!"

"Here's your airplane ticket," said Hilary Quayle.

2

I knew damn well I'd end up flying to Atlanta on Saturday, but I had to lodge a protest just to keep up my end of the tug-of-war. Before I took the job, Hilary used to run through male secretaries (the only kind she would hire) like a termite in a toothpick factory. The personnel turnover came to a halt once I joined the firm.

The firm, by the way, is Hilary Ultd., Ms. Quayle's own public relations agency. Initially, she did most of the work herself and my duties consisted chiefly of running errands, answering the phone, opening the mail, and pounding out routine releases, but lately she's been giving me more responsibilities. The boss lady is a frustrated detective. In New York, though, there is an apprenticeship period that has to be worked through in order to be eligible for an investigator's license. Hilary could not fulfill the stipulation, mainly because she's so arrogant she could never get a job procuring raunchy snapshots for divorce lawyers. But she discovered that I once used to work for just that kind of sleazy operation, and the upshot was I reactivated my file and got accreditation as a private snoop. So now Hilary uses me as her eyes and ears. Because of this, she suffers me to mouth off the way I did about the trip to meet the Boulder Clan. Of course, I don't get away with much—she still pays my salary—but at least I can bitch a little without getting sacked.

Two days after she played the record for me, I parked myself in a window seat of the no-smoking section of a United jet and unfolded the itinerary Hilary had worked out after talking to Charlie Lisle, the Boulders' manager. The group was performing a series of one-nighters for a number of weeks in a six-state area throughout the South and Midwest, ending up in Nashville in time for the Country Music Awards ceremony to be telecast live from the Grand Ole Opry. I was supposed to join the tail end of the tour and stay with them until they got to Nashville, where Hilary would fly down and meet us in time for the awards broadcast. (She was too busy to come for the whole ride, and anyway, it gave her a reason to make my life gratuitously miserable.)

The Boulders, all six of them, were the latest incarnation of one of America's oldest bluegrass-singing families. Around the time that Tom Edison was pestering anyone even remotely noteworthy to preserve their voices and talents for posterity, Pappy Boulder was learning how to scratch out a tune on a homemade fiddle. A railroad engineer, he used to relax between runs by playing at hoedowns and county fairs. Eventually, he married June Starrett, eldest daughter of a country music dynasty, and the two set about raising an army of children. By the time they stopped, the couple had a roll call of twenty-eight kids, and were so poor from providing food and clothing for a score or more Boulders, that music was the only form of entertainment they could afford to while away the evening hours. The youngsters didn't mind: They learned to pick dobros, slap bass, blast mouth organs, strum jews-harps, drum on washtubs, or invent whatever other form of rustic orchestration they could master.

Though he never attracted Edison's attention, Pappy Boulder eventually began to believe his neighbors' assurances that his family could put some of the early discoveries of the recording industry to shame. So he picked out a few of the most dedicated children, trundled them off to a round of fairs and barn dances, and ended up by turning the clan's pastime into a paying business.

As the years passed, various Boulders joined and quit the family enterprise, some of them to follow their own singing careers, some to get married. The most recent information I could garner about the Clan was a capsule biography in a magazine which listed its performing members as Pappy; a son, Samson; a nephew, Brian Lucas; two daughters, Amanda and Dolly, and their respective husbands, Merrill Gannett and Josh Mackenzie. But in the time since the article had been published, I'd heard that Merrill passed away, Pappy died at the age of 90, and Amanda left the act, being replaced by one of the younger daughters, Pearl. Out of public sight for nearly two years, Amanda had recently returned as the featured singer with the family group.

I smoothed out my itinerary and studied it once more. It spanned an eight-day period and stopped in four more towns before we hit Nashville on Thursday. After that, the Clan was booked solid for the next few days with a governor's reception, dress rehearsals for the telecast, a Saturday morning press conference, and the awards ceremony itself at 9:00 P.M. that night. Hilary planned to fly in late Friday afternoon and expected me to pick her up promptly upon arrival.

Stapled to the edge of the page was a small color photo of Dolly Boulder, who was to meet me at the Atlanta airport. She was a pretty woman who looked about twenty-five years old trying to pass for eighteen. But when I read the capsule bio of the group, I was startled to learn that she was fifth down from the top of the Clan and was therefore in her early forties. Maybe the picture was an old one. Dolly had long auburn hair framing a heart-shaped face; her complexion, though delicately hued, looked healthy and her high cheekbones reflected the light. There was no trace of eyeshadow, rouge, or lipstick upon her light skin, and Dolly's thin lips curved almost imperceptibly in a ghost of a smile which suggested that she might have a subtle, well-controlled sense of humor. Yet, there was also a vague faraway quality in the stare which I couldn't quite define. It was somewhat touching and, during the long plane ride, I looked at the photo again and again.

I arrived late in the afternoon and immediately made my way to the semicircular curb in front of the airport, but Dolly wasn't there. The flight had been delayed, and I was afraid she might be driving around trying to find a place to park, but I needn't have worried. I returned to the terminal to retrieve my bags, and then waited nearly an hour before a spangled VW bus pulled up next to me. Large banners proclaimed that it was property of the Boulder Clan. The driver's door opened and Dolly hopped out.

The picture I had studied was not an old one, but it didn't do her justice; she was prettier and younger looking in person. Except for a few lines of tension around the eyes, I saw no hint of that ambivalent smile. Instead, I was greeted heartily with a broad grin and a mischievous display of dimples. Brushing a strand of hair from her eyes, Dolly looked me up and down, stuck out a hand and, introducing herself, pumped my own in a firm and friendly grip. Then she reached down to pick up my luggage. I tried to stop her, but she good-naturedly brushed me away, hefting and stowing the suitcases into the back seat. I rounded the front of the bus, held the door open for her, then retraced my steps and got in on the opposite side. She put the gear in drive and pulled smoothly into the traffic lane leading to the downtown highway.

It was a warm afternoon and the sky was a pallid white. Sunlight picked out a stark array of architectural oddities dotting the Atlanta skyline: the sports arena, the Merchandise Mart, the futuristic contours of the Regency–Hyatt House. Dolly drove carefully, eyes riveted on the road. She was barely five feet tall and sat on a cushion so she could see comfortably over the top of the dashboard.

I stared at her, mentally contrasting her with the photo. She wore a white leatherette miniskirt and boots of the same material; the latter were ornamented with gold filigree that echoed the color of her short-sleeved silk blouse. Dolly was well-developed, and as she stepped on the gas, I became keenly aware of the briefness of her skirt. The figure she boasted was worth boasting about.

"Well, what do you say?" she asked, the faintest trace of a drawl in her voice and a wry smile on her lips. "Am I as cute as I think?"

Laughing, I assured her she was everything I'd hoped for. She wrinkled up her nose, pleased, but did not turn her head away from the road.

"Have you ever heard me sing?"

"Not solo. I've heard some of the Clan's recordings, but I don't know which was your voice."

"That's not surprising. I *never* get a chance to sing by myself. I'm the best damn mandolin picker east of Bakersfield, and I do some pretty cute prancing, but I never get a solo spot." We stopped for a traffic light and she turned to me. "Would you *like* to hear me sing? I'll do a concert just for you. . . ."

I told her it was a date, and she was pleased. But then she asked me who my favorite female country singers were, and I had to admit I wouldn't know Loretta Lynn from Lynn Anderson if I was standing next to them.

Dolly made a little *moue* of good-natured displeasure. "Well," she remarked, "you'll probably get a chance to do just that Thursday night at the governor's party. They'll all be there: Johnny Cash, Loretta Lynn, Merle Haggard, Chet Atkins—you name 'em, and you'll find 'em."

"You'll have to tell me which is which, because I won't know one from the other. The only country music I ever listened to was on WWVA."

Dolly laughed, "Wheeling, West Virginia! That's my home town! When I wasn't traveling with the act, I had my ear glued to the radio listening to WWVA."

I stuck the tip of my tongue firmly between my teeth and applied pressure. I'd almost made a crack about her pet station. I realized it was going to be a hell of a week: I'd have to keep reminding myself that I was smack in the middle of aficionados who loved whatever *I* couldn't stand. I was there to do a job for Hilary, not to vent my personal opinions.

"Tell me something about yourself," I suggested. "How long have you been with the Clan?"

She didn't answer at first, and I wondered if she'd heard me. But just when I was going to ask her again, Dolly spoke, a faraway look in her eyes.

"My pappy," she said, "handed me my first mandolin when I was a little under five years old. He told me, 'Dolly, baby, you gonna learn to play this better'n anybody else in the whole country, y'understand?' And he kept at me until I did. I guess I was maybe ten or eleven when he put me in the act." She laughed briefly, stopped. "Kept a couple of miles ahead of the truant officers. Pappy taught us our lessons while we were driving to the next gig."

It was hot; circles of perspiration soaked through Dolly's blouse beneath her arms, and I realized my shirt must look the same way. I peeled off my jacket and tossed it onto the seat behind me.

"In those days," Dolly continued, "there was just me and my pappy and my sister in the group. I used to accompany her in most of the numbers she did because she wasn't any great shakes at guitar. Pappy would do a fiddlin' solo or two, and pretty soon, I put in the prancing."

That was the second time she'd used the word. I asked her what it meant.

"Well, I guess you'd call it dancing, only that's too formal because I never took a lesson in my life. I was maybe fourteen or fifteen and we were supposed to do a show at a nightclub just outside Henderson, Kentucky, over the state line. I'll never forget that place . . . it was supposed to belong to some big-time gangster and I was scared silly to go there. I thought if they didn't like us, they'd pull out Tommy guns and shoot us full of holes. I begged my pappy to cancel out, but he wouldn't pay any attention."

Shaking her head, Dolly shuddered involuntarily. Flicking the directional arrow, she turned left out of traffic onto a tree-lined, semiresidential street.

"Anyway, like I say, it was a pretty rough club, and Pappy said afterwards he was sorry he'd dragged us there. But everything went all right at first while we were doing our group numbers. And then it came time for Amanda to sing by herself. I wasn't supposed to hog the spotlight from her, so I always stood right on the far edge of stage and gave her support with my mandolin. Pappy scooted off the side of stage to grab a shot of sour mash while we were doing the first number. Amanda took a couple of bows, and while she did, this drunk . . ." Dolly grimaced, "says something to the other men at his table, then walks on over to the edge of stage, reaches up and starts pawing at me. I moved away, but my sister pushed me right on back, like I was trying to muscle in on her applause. So I figure I better start the second number and maybe he'll leave me alone. I go into the intro for Amanda's second solo, but this bastard doesn't quit. He's blowing cigar smoke at me, making my eyes smart twice as much and he's got his hand up the back of my skirt and everybody at his table is laughing and egging him on. I was scared to get fresh with him because, for all I knew, he might have a gun in his pocket. I looked around for Pappy, but he wasn't anywhere in sight. Then, all of a sudden, I get this idea . . . it's a fast upbeat number, see, so I start on prancing in time to the music all around the stage. I put on a real wide-eyed look like I was a puppet. Of course, all I wanted to do was escape from that crud feeling me up, even if I had to make an idiot of myself to do it—but then it hits me that the whole audience is starting to laugh and hoot and cheer. So I smiled even wider and started to play and prance three times as fast. My sister couldn't even keep up with the music. Well, they applauded like crazy when I was done and naturally she was furious, but my pappy was a real showman. Soon as he saw and heard the audience re-action, he says, 'Dolly, you just keep right on prancing every time we do that number!' And pretty soon, he found other places for me to put in some footwork, and I've been doing it ever since."

Depressing the brake, Dolly eased the VW bus into the driveway of a large building that looked like a community center. She pulled around to the back, parked, and shut off the ignition. "End of the line," she said. "The rest of the Clan's rehearsing inside."

Dolly explained we'd probably head on over to the motel where the Clan was staying in Dolly's own car afterwards, so we got out of the VW and transferred the bags to the trunk of a yellow Thunderbird. I tried to carry my luggage again, but she beat me to it and made me walk beside her empty-handed, feeling foolish.

She dimpled up her face and pointed an admonitory finger in my direction without releasing her grip on my suitcase. "Now don't forget," she said, "we've got a date, the two of us."

"A date?"

"There, now!" she said, pretending pique. "You *did* forget already! You were going to listen to me sing."

I apologized and asked when she would like me to hear her.

"How about tonight? After the show, you and me can go out and have a couple of drinks, then I'll drive us back to the motel, and I'll get out my mandolin and give you a command performance."

I had no doubt of the innocence of the proposal, but its directness surprised me. I wondered how the notion would sit with Josh. "Look," I told Dolly, "that all sounds fine to me, but won't your husband mind the two of us going off alone?"

We were at the back door of the building. I opened it, but Dolly didn't go through. She stared at me curiously, and the enigmatic expression of the photograph appeared fleetingly in her eyes.

"I haven't got a husband," she said, turning and walking through the door.

3

Dolly frowned as we entered the auditorium. There should have been five people rehearsing onstage, but instead we found only three—two men and a young girl who, by process of elimination, had to be Pearl.

Sitting down in the first row, I watched while Dolly picked up her mandolin and joined the others in a countrified version of "Yellow Bird." The four voices blended nicely and Dolly pranced in place, smiling like a china doll and projecting a dainty cuteness without becoming cloying. She was certainly the focus of attention, at least during that number.

Her sister, several inches taller, was a blonde who used too much makeup. She wore a black sweater and scarlet slacks, both too small—so tight that her bra and the edge of her panties showed through. The effect was less stimulating than she might have wished.

At the end of "Yellow Bird," Pearl walked to center stage, readjusted the guitar strap on her shoulder, and began picking out a blues tune. The bass player—a dark-haired character with glasses, serious expression, and a bit of a paunch—

set a deliberate rhythm beneath the melody, while the second man—a muscular giant with a shock of unruly black hair—doubled the main subject on dobro. Pearl began to sing.

"What the hell is going on?" Dolly interrupted, setting down her mandolin and staring at them in amazement. The music stopped.

"I'm taking Amanda's place," Pearl said, somewhat belligerently.

"Why?" Dolly asked. "Where's Josh?"

"Had to drive Amanda to the airport," said the big man. "Must've been heading over while you were coming back. Show her the telegram, Brian." He spoke the last to the bass player, who produced a folded yellow square of paper and handed it to Dolly. She took it and began to read.

Pearl nodded, and the three began strumming the blues number again.

The telegram came from Nashville, where Charlie Lisle, the Clan's manager, had gone a few days earlier to work out last-minute details for the group's guest shot on the NBC telecast. In the message, he told Amanda to catch the first plane out of Atlanta and join him at the Grand Ole Opry. Pearl was supposed to fill in for her sister on the road.

The reason for the substitution must be important, I thought, listening to Pearl sing, because she had a long way to go to rival her sister as a vocalist.

When the rehearsal was over, Dolly officially introduced me to the others, though, by then, I knew which was which. Cousin Brian was quiet and unsmiling. Samson, the giant, second oldest of the Boulder siblings (a year younger than Amanda), had huge hands, a bull neck, and stood well over

six feet tall. He moved awkwardly and sounded angry whenever he spoke.

The five of us headed upstairs to a combination recreation
hall-cafeteria in the community center. It was a large, chilly
room with a polished floor and sticky formica-top tables.
As we entered, some teenagers playing shuffleboard by the
wall looked up and gawked in admiration at the Clan. A
couple of them came over asking for autographs, which the
four entertainers signed while standing in line waiting to
fill their trays with food.

We sat at a large table off to one side. There wasn't much
time for supper because the girls had to get back downstairs soon to make up. What conversation there was
centered on Charlie Lisle's calling Amanda to Nashville. It
was a family caucus; I ate and listened.

"Charlie's an S.O.B.," Pearl said, her mouth full of bread.
"I think he's pulling something lousy."

"He's okay," Samson grumbled.

"Well, sure, *you'd* think so," Pearl sneered.

"What the hell's that supposed to mean?"

"Anything you want!"

"The two of you pipe down," Dolly said, puckering her
lips in annoyance. Brian turned to Samson and asked what
he thought Lisle was planning.

"I don't know," the large man said, "but he's not trying
anything dirty. Maybe he wants to get the numbers straight
for the governor's party and the broadcast."

"That's dumb!" Pearl said loudly. "That's real dumb!
Charlie could call us on the phone for that."

"Don't call me dumb," Samson growled, tearing a bite
out of a chicken leg.

She didn't heed his warning. Raising her voice, she
taunted him: "Well, you *are* dumb! And don't hush me up,

Miss Prancy Legs, because you know he's dumb, too! Dumb old Alvin!"

Samson rose, reached across the table and grabbed Pearl's hair, twisting it so hard that she was yanked halfway across the table. She yelped.

Dolly jumped up and slapped his hand hard, forcing him to release Pearl.

"Leave her alone, Samson," she ordered. "Pearl's the dumb one, calling people names. *Now sit!*"

"Look what that bastard did to my hair!" Pearl wailed. Dolly rounded on her with a vehemence I never would have imagined her capable of.

"You close that stupid mouth!" In spite of her fury, Dolly's voice was hushed. "What's the matter with you?" she asked, gesturing to the other side of the cafeteria. "Don't you see we're in public? We're the lovin Boulder Clan, *remember?!*"

She sat down and attacked her food with short, vicious jabs of the fork. Nobody said anything for a long time.

Gathering up nerve, Pearl finally broke the silence. "Well, if anybody's interested, I'll tell you what *I* think."

No one spoke.

"I'll tell you, anyway! *I* think Charlie fixed up a solo number on that TV special for Amanda. What do you say to *that?*"

Dolly and Samson looked at one another. Then Dolly turned to Pearl and asked why she thought so.

"Because that's the only reason I can figure why it'd be so important for Amanda to drop everything and fly to Nashville."

Samson snorted indignantly. Dolly toyed with her food. Several minutes passed.

At last, Brian asked Pearl if she had a suitable solo ballad ready in case of an encore that night. "How about 'I'll Never Call You Sweetheart Again'?" he suggested.

"Very funny," Pearl sniffed, her lips curling in a mirthless smile. "I could substitute real good on that song. All I'd have to do is not sing it."

"You damn well better not," a new voice said. "Your sister'd break your ass."

I turned and saw a tall, lanky man of about thirty-five with sleek brown hair plastered down in a thick back-parting and a mouth that hung open in a perpetual grin. He lounged carelessly with hands in the pockets of his blue jeans, and wore a pair of dark glasses pushed onto his forehead.

The women rose and he put his arms around their shoulders. Dolly introduced me to Josh.

"Amanda get off all right?" Samson asked. Josh nodded casually.

"Josh," Pearl asked, looking up at him, "why do you think Charlie had Amanda light out for Nashville all of a sudden?"

"Never mind," he drawled, patting her shoulder with a big paw. "We've got a surprise for you once we get to Nashville, but I'm not saying word one about it till then."

And he didn't, either—though both women tried to worm it out of him.

After the show that night, Dolly complained of a headache, so we agreed to postpone our private concert. I went to my motel room and entered my first impressions of the Clan in a notebook. Then I tried to watch a late movie on television—but I got fed up with the local commercials in a half-hour and decided to turn in.

As I was switching off the set, I heard a tap at the door. Opening it, I found Dolly standing there, a tense, pinched expression on her face. One hand was slanted across her forehead, while she carried her mandolin case in the other. I asked whether she still had a headache, but she claimed to feel a lot better and asked whether it was too late for a nightcap and a couple of songs, after all.

"Of course not," I told her. "Come on in."

Later on, I decided that Dolly could interpret a song much better than her younger sister, yet she didn't measure up to Amanda. But I didn't tell her that.

4

In the next four days, I saw a lot more of Dolly than anyone else, a fact that would have annoyed Hilary, who'd sent
me to get acquainted with all of the Boulders. A two-person
PR agency is necessarily limited in the number of clients it
can effectively service, and the boss wanted me to find out
whether we'd have any undue personality conflicts in case
she decided to represent the family; once they got to Nashville and started rehearsing for the awards ceremony, I
wouldn't have much of a chance to talk with them.

But there wasn't a lot of available time while they were
traveling, either. When they weren't busy rehearsing, they
were performing; or if they weren't doing a show, they'd be
packing up for the next one. Meals were rushed, and there
was little time for sleep. Anybody not driving would sack
out during between-show trips.

To make things tougher, we split into three parties during
the daytime. Samson took the instruments and audio equip-
ment in the VW bus, barreling over hairpin turns that
hovered above swift-running streams. Josh followed in a
bright gold Lincoln, speeding dangerously over the narrow

country roads, and Pearl rode with him. I spelled Dolly frequently at the wheel of her car, and Brian rode in back, saying nothing, but then, he never did say much.

Still, I talked a little with the others. On Monday, when we only had a short hop between Franklin, North Carolina, and Cherokee, Samson and I had a couple of beers and he told me about his early days as a tent-show strong man, when he changed his name from Alvin to Samson.

I also spent a little time with Pearl, and found that she'd studied voice in New York, where she'd lived a couple of years while trying to break into musical comedy. When it became obvious that jobs weren't going to materialize overnight, it occurred to her that it wouldn't hurt to pile up professional credits working in the family act; after Merrill Gannett died and Amanda quit the Clan, Pearl gladly took the solo spot when Pappy offered it to her.

The old man apparently was snowed by the fact that Pearl had professional polish, but as soon as Pappy died Charlie Lisle began urging Amanda to come out of retirement . . . a fact that accounted for his lack of popularity with Pearl Boulder.

Dolly didn't talk much about her younger sister, and I figured she resented Pearl's voice lessons. Dolly was sensitive about her lack of education. She told me that she planned to go back to school someday.

"After I graduate, you know what I'll do?" she asked me once, resting against my shoulder as I piloted the Thunderbird past a long line of weather-worn shacks dotting the highway. "I'm going to write books."

"What kind?"

"Mysteries. Thrillers. Girls that get tangled up with a man who lives in an old house out in the middle of nowhere—you know. I've got plenty of ideas."

She told me a few of her plots, and I pretended they were good.

I was sure Amanda would be in Charlie Lisle's office Thursday, but I was wrong—I didn't meet her till that night.

We drove into Nashville a little before noon. The Clan headed straight over to the manager's; I confirmed the reservations at the Ramada, then followed in a taxi.

Lisle's office occupied the top story of a three-level brick building on Sixteenth Avenue South, Nashville's "Music Row." The reception area was a barren green shell with nothing to look at but superannuated album covers on the wall and a ditto secretary seated behind a flimsy metal desk. He took my name and explained that Lisle was in conference and could not be disturbed.

I didn't have long to wait. After a few minutes, the inner office door opened and Brian Lucas walked out, a sour smile twisting one corner of his mouth. He shook his head as he met my stare, and without saying a word, disappeared down the stairs. He was followed by a silent Dolly, who walked past without seeing me. Samson and Pearl were next. She hissed something beneath her breath as they emerged and Samson pushed her roughly aside; Pearl uttered an unlady-like remark and left. As soon as she did, Samson turned and reentered Lisle's office, shutting the door. I could hear the big man raising his voice several times in the next few minutes. At last, he banged the door back on its hinges and stamped downstairs, livid with rage.

"Come in and sit down," a weary voice told me. I entered a small room and sat in a leatherette swivel chair, noticing that neither Josh nor Amanda had participated in the family conclave.

Lisle was a fussy man in his early forties. His bald head

was surrounded by a grizzled tuft that looked like steel wool, and his mouth, flabby-lipped, puckered in a mirthless half-smile; the teeth that showed were discolored. He wore a drab suit that matched the pepper-and-salt fringe of hair.

Shaking his head as he took a seat behind a chrome-and-plastic desk, Lisle murmured, "Samson never knows how to keep emotions out of practical matters." He spoke precisely, enunciating each syllable as if he were tasting every letter. "I only wish he realized there's nothing personal. . . ." He shrugged, dismissing the train of thought. "I'm sorry *you* had to become involved in all this."

Not knowing what *this* referred to, I told him I was ready to set up press contacts for the Clan or do anything else to help out, but any serious business talks would have to wait for Hilary to arrive the next night.

Lisle's eyes had a habit of darting nervously around the room; and they shifted now to a spot on the wall two feet above my head. "We have a problem," he said. "You see, there isn't going to be any more Clan."

"There *isn't?*" I asked, raising an eyebrow.

"Amanda doesn't need the rest of them." He spoke with great deliberation, weighing every word. "There is no profit left in trying to book a six-person act. It costs too much, even at scale. When Pappy was alive, it was a different story, of course. Bad as he was, he was an institution. . . ."

"So that's why they left here looking like the tail end of a wake."

He shook his head slowly. "I did not tell them my eventual intention. I only said that Amanda has a solo on the awards telecast and will do the same song tonight at the governor's instead of the group number that they had planned. That was enough." His mouth turned down in a distasteful frown. "*They* . . . will never understand I have

to do it this way. It's poor business for me to keep them together."

"And where does *my* . . . Ms. Quayle's firm come in?"

"I thought you might be interested in representing Amanda
Boulder alone."

I didn't like it, but I said we might. "What about the press
brunch Saturday?" I asked. "Isn't it pointless?"

"No. That's when I will announce Amanda's intention to
go solo." Lisle drummed his fingers on the desktop. I noticed the high gloss on his nails and ornate rings on each
hand. "After this morning," he continued dolefully, "I can
just imagine how pleasant it will be telling them the rest
of the news. . . ."

"Speaking of news," I remarked, "Josh said he had a surprise to spring on the Clan in Nashville. Does it concern
what you've just been telling me?"

The manager looked out the window at the traffic on Sixteenth Avenue. After a few seconds, he shrugged, murmur-
ing, "Why don't you ask Josh?"

That ended my meeting with Lisle.

5

I couldn't ask Josh because I couldn't find him. On the road, he always was wherever I wasn't, and in Nashville, I didn't have a clue to his whereabouts. But I found out all about his surprise that night at the governor's when I heard Amanda sing for the second time.

The rest of the family went on ahead early. I caught a limousine provided by Goodfellow Industries, sponsors of the NBC telecast. It was a drive of about six miles south-west of center city. The driver turned in at the gates of a graceful Georgian-style manor set in ten acres of well-tended park. Standing at the door were the governor and his wife, smiling with real professional style as they person-ally greeted every guest. Inside, the place was immaculate and gleaming. It was an impressive building, but living in it must have been as cozy as having cocktails in the Library of Congress.

The central reception hall, graced by the ascending curve of a spiral staircase, was jammed with celebrities, journal-ists, visiting golf pros, area legislators, and local socialites. High-power lights had been set up by the mobile unit of a local TV station, and it was hot. I made my way to the rear of the house, where most of the action was centered. Passing through the middle arch of a triple-clustered portico, I entered a paved courtyard where tables of liquor and food had been set. It was warm out there, too, and the press of bodies didn't help. The din of voices was capped by a cacophony of fiddling. The musician, a man with long black hair, stood on a platform at the far end of the patio. I couldn't find the Boulders, so I made my way to the liquor table, vainly hoping to find some Bushmill's in sour mash territory.

In the next half-hour, I managed to meet ten country-western singers, only three of whom I'd ever heard before, and was introduced to the head of Nashville's third most prominent family. By ten o'clock, I was worn out from side-stepping invitations to name my country-music preferences. I leaned against a pillar and narrowly avoided dousing Glen Campbell with Bourbon when a Nashville councilman plowed into me en route to a TV camera pointed at one of his political rivals.

The crowd had just finished laughing at some of Mel Tillis's drolleries when I spotted Dolly mounting the steps of the platform with the rest of the Clan behind her, carrying their instruments. I worked my way forward to get a better vantage point, and while I was busy shoving shoulders and dodging feet, I temporarily lost sight of the platform. I heard Josh over the mike saying hello to the governor and his guests; then he introduced Amanda. After a brief round of applause, the Clan struck up the introduction to her song.

A sudden murmur sprang up, but was quickly suppressed by a chorus of hushes, when Amanda sang:

I have seen your eyes and know that they are yearning,
I have fled them down the years, but all in vain. . . .

I reached the front by the time she got to the chorus and saw Amanda. I'd imagined she would be beautiful but was off base. She had lifeless brown hair chopped in a Prince Valiant cut. Her figure was straight up and down, and the dress she wore looked like it had been made on a kitchen table in a bad light. But none of that mattered. When she sang, Amanda was suddenly quite desirable. The pain in her green eyes, the eloquent anguish that throbbed in her voice begged the listener to comfort an inconsolable sorrow.

The Clan played a short break before she sang the last verse. I could see no trace of emotion in their faces. Dolly might have been a puppet mechanically brushing her arm against the mandolin. Pearl wore a pasted-on smile that was out of keeping with the melancholy nature of the number. The men merely looked stolid.

It happened in the final verse. Amanda made a change in the lyric of the next-to-last line, and the audience again whispered.

Well, I cry each time I dream I hear you singing,
Though the pain I feel is nothing like your pain.
But I'll find another love to ease the stinging
And I'll never call you sweetheart again.

The song ended. Before anyone could applaud, Amanda spoke in a husky, intimate voice. "I guess," she said, "that you all know what that song means to me. I can never say how much your good wishes have meant to me in the last few years. . . ." Closing her eyes, she took a deep breath. The patio was so still it might have been deserted.

She addressed the audience as if every member were a

personal friend. "You know I'll never *ever* forget—but I want you to be the first to share my . . . my happiness, too . . . and. . . ."

Amanda faltered, gesturing helplessly. Josh strode forward and grabbed the mike. His eternal grin was broader than ever, and he hugged Amanda tightly round her shoulders. "What she means to say is that me and Amanda are going to hitch up together!"

No one moved for a second or two. Then a flashbulb popped, and Dolly stepped forward and yelled, "Come on, let's hear it for 'em!" She started the applause, and the mob took it up. A barrage of photographers lit the scene with artificial light. Dolly turned, whispering to the rest of the Clan, and the group started to play a bluegrass version of "Here Comes the Bride." The audience clapped in time. Pearl, no longer wearing the pasted-on smile, strummed vigorously and sang. Dolly pranced in place, and everyone except Amanda looked happy.

After the reception, I rode back to the Ramada in the VW with Samson and Brian.

"How come I got the impression that the audience was surprised to hear Amanda sing that song?" I asked.

"Because they *were* surprised," Brian said.

"Why? It's her latest hit."

"Yes. But after she recorded it, she told Charlie Lisle she'd never sing it again."

Up till then, Samson had said nothing. But when he heard Lisle's name, he mumbled something under his breath. He never would have said it over a microphone.

6

In 1885, when buggies still rattled noisily over Nashville's dusty roads, a preacher by the name of Sam Jones came to town to stage a prayer meeting. He was a hellfire-and-brimstone evangelist from Georgia who prided himself on his ability to literally scare the Devil out of the most impenitent of sinners. Not far away from where Jones pitched his tent, a riverboat gambling casino was moored on the banks of the Cumberland. Its owner, Tom Ryman, liked to "bust up" prayer meetings.

But the gambler didn't scare the revivalist, who regarded him as a challenge. Jones had an invitation for Ryman to come hear his sermon delivered directly to the riverboat.

Ryman was amused. Rounding up a crew of roustabouts, he stomped into the tent that night, ready to stage a lusty brawl, but Jones was ready for him. Pointing an accusatory finger at the gambler, he hurled brimstone, Demon Rum, and Motherhood straight at him. Ryman didn't have a chance; Jones soon reduced him to a weeping penitent. The only "busting up" he did that night was aboard his own riverboat. He took an ax to the gaming tables and chopped them into kindling.

Over the next decade and a half, Ryman and Jones became fast friends. Together, the unlikely pair worked mightily to build a revival hall on Nashville's Summer Street. Raising funds for the costly project a little at a time, it took them until the turn of the century before the Union Gospel Tabernacle received official incorporation papers from the state of Tennessee. Tom Ryman died a few years later and some four thousand mourners attended his funeral. Sam Jones hurried up from Atlanta to officiate, and when the preacher suggested the name of the hall be changed to the Ryman Auditorium, everyone rose in agreement.

Four decades passed. During that time, Summer Street became Fifth Avenue, and the Ryman turned into a temple of culture. All the leading artists of the day—from Kreisler, Elman, and Nijinsky to Tetrazzini, Maude Adams and Marian Anderson—gave concerts at the famous auditorium. In one memorable year, Nashville's elite jammed beneath the building's peaked roof on four separate occasions to hear Caruso, Galli–Curci and John McCormack, and to watch and wonder at the striking new dance notions of Isadora Duncan.

But there was also something else happening in Nashville in the first half of the twentieth century. It had little to do with the highbrow goings-on at the Ryman at first. In 1925, a local radio station (WSM) with a powerful broadcasting signal began presenting a weekly "hoedown" of country music live each Saturday night. Known as the "Grand Ole Opry," it was everything that the Ryman wasn't.

"Thuh Opry" began to attract the attention of rural Americans in practically every state of the union. Each Saturday night, Stromberg Carlsons, Philcos, and even homemade crystal sets sought out 650 on the dial. Nashville became a medium for uniting displaced farmers of the Depression, migrant workers fleeing the Dust Bowl, backwoods and mountain kin in Appalachia and the Blue Ridge. The Grand Ole Opry, a musical reminiscence of "home" with its clear-cut moral values, was soon a national institution, and it became the dream of every rustic clan to pile into the family jalopy someday and see Minnie Pearl or Tex Ritter or Carson Robison perform live at the Opry. Teen-agers yearned to sing on the show themselves, pouring out their private frustrations in songs that might turn them into millionaires overnight.

The Opry and the Ryman were as unlikely a pair as Jones and Ryman, but they also eventually got together. In 1941, WSM acquired the venerable auditorium and began broadcasting the country-music show from it. Several years later, the station's owner, National Life and Accident Insurance Company, bought the building outright and changed its name to the Grand Ole Opry House.

On Friday morning, there was already a long line of tourists stretching down the Opry's front steps and up the sloping sidewalk of Fifth Avenue. Samson turned the VW into an alleyway running alongside the building and pulled into the back lot.

It was a hot morning; the air shimmered. The Clan unloaded the musical instruments and headed for the stage door, but a small horde of kids, women in print dresses, and thickset men in blue jeans converged on the Boulders, and the family spent several minutes in an orgy of autographing and down-home talk. Though the dress rehearsal was already in progress, none of the Clan showed any sign of impatience at the delay.

The inside of the Ryman was all wooden seats and timber paneling. There was no air-conditioning, and the place was stuffy; technicians sweated in jackets and ties, while celebrities were dressed more sensibly in open-collared shirts and jeans. Five cameras with NBC call letters emblazoned on their sides were mounted on a temporary apron that had been built out from the permanent Opry stage. A border of footlights surrounded the apron and flared brightly whenever the cameras ran. Cables snaked over the floor and up the aisles, making the place a network of obstacles. High above the broad spread of seats hung a timbered balcony, suspended in place by numerous steel beams.

The auditorium was filled with network officials, PR men, and the technical staff, all milling about, and country-music personalities, all sitting still. The press reps busily ferried an army of reporters and columnists to the various celebrities, motionless islands in the sea of activity.

In one corner, June Cash sat with her husband and held a small child on her lap. Nearby, George Lindsay chatted with "Tennessee" Ernie Ford. From where I stood, I could hear Porter Wagoner (whom I had met at the governor's party) telling a reporter about his early days as a stock boy. "My boss," he said to the journalist, "bought a fifteen-minute spot on local radio. I sang on the program—but at the end of the day, I still had to put up my guitar and straighten the stock. . . ."

Charley Pride took his place onstage beneath a hanging boom-mike and began to rehearse "Is Anybody Goin to San Antone?" The talk died down and I heard some of the other singers shushing the reporters and PR men so they could listen to Pride. I could see why his colleagues gave him their attention: He was an electrifying showman.

Pride stood on the forestage, which was bare except for a lectern off to one side where the MC announced the acts and introduced those who would present the awards. A pitcher of water and a glass rested on top of the podium. Behind the singer, a diaphanous blue curtain divided the stage horizontally; on its other side, the band sat and played on a high platform.

The Boulder Clan followed Pride, and their rehearsal of "Rockland County Prison" took up the rest of the morning. When a lunch break was announced, the family decided to eat together. We all climbed into the three vehicles and headed out to a Mexican restaurant that Dolly had recommended.

The waitress seated us at a long table, with Josh and Amanda at one end and me and Dolly at the other. Samson was on my left and Pearl sat beside Josh. Samson opened the conversation by asking the betrothed couple where they were going on their honeymoon.

"We aren't kids," Josh laughed. "Amanda and me are working out some numbers so we can take 'em right out."

"Charlie hasn't come up with any new dates," Pearl complained. "Where do you think you're going to take these numbers?"

"It's like this," he said. "Amanda and me are going on a tour of our own." Everyone stared at him. Knives and forks were replaced on the table. Amanda looked down at her hands, resting in her lap.

After a long moment of silence, Dolly asked, "When did you two decide on this?"

"I've been meaning to talk to Charlie about it," Josh said casually, rolling a forkful of beans in a flour tortilla. "I figure we'll take off right after the wedding."

"And when's that?" Pearl asked.

"Next week," Josh replied, chewing his food. "I want to follow right up on Amanda singing on the telecast."

"Charlie won't go for this!" Samson growled. "What the hell are *we* supposed to do?"

"Oh, hell, boy, you just keep right on working as a quartet. Let Pearl go back to singing the solos."

There was no more talk on the subject, but Josh got dirty looks from time to time from everybody at the table, including Amanda.

The women left early so Amanda could rehearse her solo. The rest of us sat around finishing a gallon of beer, which we really needed after consuming so many enchiladas. Samson asked Josh a few questions about his future plans, while Brian, as usual, said nothing.

When we returned to the Opry, the auditorium was practically deserted. The other entertainers were probably still at lunch, so the reporters were also absent. Amanda was onstage and the camera crew was busy setting up angles and shots for "I'll Never Call You Sweetheart Again." The band, back from lunch, had already taken its place behind the divider curtain.

Josh, Samson, and Brian returned to their common dressing room, where they were supposed to meet Charlie Lisle. I remained in the auditorium to watch the rehearsal. The band played Amanda's introduction and she made her entrance wearing a pale green cocktail dress that might have been stylish twenty years earlier. The cameras pivoted and followed as she reached center stage, stopping under the boom at a spot where the floor manager had chalked a green line. She began to sing.

I slumped into my seat, disgusted. The previous week had been a big waste of time. The Clan was going to split up and Lisle would only be managing Amanda. And Josh. Should I recommend that Hilary represent them? Much as I admired Amanda, I didn't like scrapping the rest of the family.

"Hold it, Miss Boulder," the voice of the program director droned over a loudspeaker, "let's readjust that shot." The director spoke from a control booth where he monitored a bank of tiny TV screens corresponding to the images on each camera. He was invisible, but at his command, all progress stopped and artists and technicians backtracked like a movie being rewound. There was a moment of silence. Amanda stood near the lectern, waiting patiently. She poured herself a drink of water.

I thought about Hilary. What the hell was I going to tell her that afternoon when I picked her up at the airport? She would be sore to learn I'd accomplished nothing meaningful all week. Even though it wasn't my fault, I knew her temper and—

A sharp crash caused me to look up. The glass of water Amanda had been drinking was shattered on the floor. Her hands clutched tightly about her throat, and there was a horrified look in her eyes. She swayed.

"What's the trouble, Miss Boulder?" the director's unemotional voice asked over the loudspeaker.

Amanda's face was hideously contorted, and as she doubled over, I saw her raise a hand to her lips, trying to claw the taste from her mouth. Her shoulders heaved convulsively. There was a spot of red on her lips.

"Miss Boulder," the director repeated, *"what's the matter?"* One of the cameramen looked around the side of his instrument, a worried expression on his face.

Amanda tried to speak, but couldn't. She stumbled to the side of the platform and fell to her knees. I jumped up, leaped onstage, and pulled a cameraman away from his post. "Quick," I ordered, "call for a doctor." He spoke a few words into his headset, hung it over the camera's directional arm, and hurried out to a side corridor where the Opry's business office was located. Running to Amanda, I tried to help her to her feet. Her face was pale and she shivered uncontrollably.

"Gene, what's wrong?!"

I turned. Dolly was standing in the wings, a stricken look on her face. She stared at her sister.

"Something was in the water," I told her. "We'd better help her lie down."

"Her dressing room is on the other side," Dolly said. We crossed the stage and went down a short flight of stairs to the corridor where the dressing rooms were located. Amanda whimpered as we dragged her along.

Dolly kicked open a door halfway down the hall. It was a long, narrow room, with a wooden bench butted against a makeup table that ran the whole length of one wall. We lowered Amanda onto a hard cot in the corner.

"Quick!" Dolly said, "get the others!" She pressed my hand urgently, and I ran out to find the men's dressing room.

I had no trouble guessing which room it was—I could hear the ruckus ten feet away. Pushing open the door, I saw Samson Boulder and Charlie Lisle fighting—if you can call anything so one-sided a fight. The giant had his hands wrapped around Lisle's neck and was slamming the manager against the wall. Josh and Brian each had one of Samson's arms and were trying to pull him away from the manager.

"Let go, you frigging bastard!" Josh yelled, but Samson flicked him off with incredible ease. Josh piled back into him, trying to get his arm locked around Samson's throat, but it was a tough trick because of the inequality of height.

"Knock it off," I ordered. "Amanda's been poisoned."

I didn't think they heard at first, but Samson let go of Lisle and spun around. They all stared at me blankly for a few seconds, then Josh cursed, and suddenly everybody was talking. Samson ran past me, then stopped, realizing he didn't know where he was going.

I explained the situation briefly, then led the way to Amanda's dressing room, turning at the last to prevent them from crowding in on her. Dolly was sitting on the cot, dabbing at her sister's face with a cloth. Amanda's eyes were closed and she was moaning.

"Give her a shot of whiskey," Josh suggested, but Lisle advised against it. Samson thought she should be forced to vomit.

I ran back onstage to see whether a doctor was on the way. A thought struck me en route, and I grabbed the headset hanging from the vacant camera and put it on. The director told me to get the hell off, but I repeated my instructions.

"You're nuts!" his voice said in my ear. "I've got a show to put on."

"I don't give a damn. Kill the rehearsal."

"I can't! Who's going to pay the crew? *My* budget won't cover the overtime!"

"Just keep people off the stage," I said. "Make certain nobody touches that pitcher or the glass on the floor. Don't let them clean up the pieces." I took off the headset before he could register any further protest.

Back in the dressing room, Dolly was cleaning up. Amanda had vomited, and she was soaking in sweat. Spittle coursed down the sides of her lolling mouth and there were tears in her eyes; she writhed in pain. When the doctor arrived a few minutes later, he took one look at the sick woman and sent Josh off to phone for an ambulance.

Dolly began to weep, and I told Brian to get her the hell out of there; then Samson and I hefted the cot and began carrying it toward the rear exit.

"What's happening?"

Looking up, we saw Pearl standing in the wings. Lisle told her that Amanda was very sick.

"Yeah?" she asked eagerly. "Then what happens to her solo on the show? Can I do it?"

I thought Samson might murder her, but he growled instead, "Move out of the way, you stupid bitch."

We got Amanda to the back of the auditorium as the ambulance pulled up. A pair of orderlies placed her on a stretcher, put it in the vehicle and set off for the hospital with Samson and Brian following in the VW. I went back inside the Opry House.

I had a call to make to the police.

7

I sat on the wooden bench so long that my spine developed lateral indentations. Samson was smarter—he paced back and forth from one hospital-green wall to the other.

"I used to settle fights for her, even though she was older," he told me, breaking stride momentarily before resuming the pacing. "One snotty bastard called her flat-chested Mandy, and she moped in her room for two days—crying. I broke his nose."

He'd been aiming recollections at me for an hour and a half, and they were starting to come around for the second time. I'd already learned Amanda's preference in colors, clothing, sports, and ten other things, and I knew what her worst school subjects were. I had a full account of how Samson had been her best man.

"She was crazy about Merrill ever since the Gannetts moved in down the valley from us," Samson said. "She nearly went out of her mind when he died."

The door opened and a police sergeant stuck in his head, pointed at Samson and withdrew. My companion followed him out.

The only member of the Clan who hadn't been questioned yet was Dolly, but she was in no state to be bothered. She'd gone to the hospital to check on Amanda, which had been a mistake. When Dolly arrived at the station house, she had red circles under her eyes and her face was pallid.

I was in the waiting room with Pearl, Samson, and Brian when Dolly walked in, blinking to fight back tears. She swayed in the doorway. "Amanda's dead," she said. "There was so much *pain*."

Dolly began to shake hysterically, and I put my arm around her. She dropped her head against my shoulder and gained control of herself long enough to look at the others. *"How?"* she asked. "How could anybody pick such an awful way to kill her?!" Then she began to cry again.

Josh came in a moment later from being questioned, and we had to send Dolly back to the Ramada with him.

By the time they got around to calling me for questioning it was late in the afternoon. I stepped into a small room filled with filing cabinets and a nicked cherrywood desk. A chunky deputy sheriff in a tan uniform stood up and shook hands with me, motioning me to a seat near the door. I'd met him earlier. His name was Joe Cass.

The first order of business was to record routine information on official forms . . . name, residence, occupation, relationship (if any) to the deceased, and so on. It took several minutes before Cass put the pencil down, folded his hands in his lap and stared in my direction.

"I want to thank you for squaring things away at the Opry," he said. "How'd you know we wouldn't want anything touched? Read a lot of detective stories?"

I explained that I had a New York private investigator's license.

Cass nodded. "I know. I checked."

"Then why did you ask?"

"To see how honest you were." He scratched the side of his cheek, contemplating me in silence for a long time.

"Look," he said, abruptly, "this goddamn case is a pain." I nodded, not knowing what to say.

"It's the family. They don't open up. Loyalty of kin, distrust of authority."

"What do you want me to do?"

"You've been with them. What can you tell me?"

"I'm an outsider, too; I don't know all that much. But they're public property, there must be millions of words. . . ."

He waved a hand deprecatingly, and, reaching into a drawer, pulled out a sheaf of press clippings and slid them across the desk. "There's nothing recent except the stuff about Amanda joining the group again."

I rooted through the pile, but couldn't do it justice in a few minutes. Cass said I could have stats made.

"The thing I have to figure," he said, "is who had the opportunity to slip something into the pitcher."

"What kind of poison was it?"

"The lab hasn't called in yet."

"Well, everybody knew the rehearsal schedule," I remarked, "so anyone who walked onstage during the lunch break could have dosed the water."

"From twelve to one," said Cass, "there was hardly anybody around. The camera crew and director were on their lunch break. How about the Boulders?"

I told him about the Clan's movements from morning to postlunch. I couldn't remember anyone but Amanda going near the water pitcher.

"How about motive?" he asked.

I spread my hands, palms up. "That all depends how strong a reason you consider professional jealousy. Nobody was happy about Amanda getting the solo spot."

The deputy took a deep breath. "That's *plenty* reason in Nashville for knocking off a relative." He wagged a finger at me. "I rent out the top story of my house. A lot of buck-toothed kids have stayed over the years, up in my attic. It's the same pattern—no job, no letters home, no meals except a bite to keep up energy to sing. Same shoes and shorts and socks till they peel off in patches. They walk everywhere—from Tootsie's and the Opry to Music Row, where the secretaries smile and shoo 'em off. Then home, five hours of sleep, and another trudge downtown. . . . And what for? So they can ride around in big cars wearing shiny suits and boots and buy ranch houses for families they'd never get to see because they'd be out on the road most of the year—singing about loneliness, and taking pills to have enough energy for the next show." He nodded. "Oh, yeah—they'd kill all right,—if they really thought it'd help them get there. . . ."

The phone rang. Cass spoke into it, then listened carefully before replacing the receiver. There was a peculiar look in his eyes.

"Tell me about lunch," he demanded. "What did Amanda have to eat?"

I shrugged. "I didn't watch her, bite for bite. But she must have had what everyone else did—combination plates. Tacos, burritos, enchiladas, tostadas, tamales, refried beans, and green chili."

"Anything else?"

"Flour tortillas."

"Did they serve everything separately?"

"No. We all had individual plates. The food came on big platters and we served ourselves from them."

"Do you remember what she drank?"

"Coke, I think. Why?"

Cass shook his head. "Christ, this is a real pisser. That was the lab. We won't know what finished her without an autopsy."

"How come? Didn't they analyze the contents of the pitcher?"

He nodded. "Clean. No trace of poison."

"So?" I said, "the poison must have been in the glass, the one that got broken."

"Negative," the deputy replied. "There was enough of the base of the tumbler left to scrape up a liquid sample. That's clean, too."

It didn't make sense. If she'd been poisoned at lunch, then we *all* would have been. What about earlier? But how could anything so deadly be so slow-acting? No—I'd seen the stuff hit her right after she drank from the pitcher. The violence of the reaction was unmistakable. The poison *had* to be in the water.

But it wasn't.

Cass and I spent a few minutes reconstructing the Clan's later movements. After lunch, I reminded him, the men had gone to their common dressing room to meet with Lisle, after the women already had returned to the Opry. Pearl said she hadn't seen anybody near the podium, but that didn't prove anything, since she was a suspect herself.

"Look," Cass said, "we're wasting time trying to decide who could have dosed the water. The lab just told us the water was clean."

"All right. What do you suggest?"

"Damned if I know."

"How long before we get results of the autopsy?"

"Late tonight, maybe not till tomorrow." He shrugged.

I couldn't think of anything else. I told Cass I'd phone if I got any bright ideas; meanwhile, I wanted to get back to the Ramada and dip into the press file. We shook hands and I left.

Out in the parking lot, I was glad to see that Dolly's car was still there. She'd given me a spare key, so I got in and started heading toward the motel when, all of a sudden, it hit me. I looked at my wristwatch and felt sick.

My God! I thought, *Cass is going to have another murder on his hands.*

I'd forgotten to pick up Hilary at the airport.

My luck stayed lousy. Hilary's flight arrived ahead of schedule, and she was no longer at the airport. That was even worse for me. I drove back to the Ramada and was greeted by a curt message waiting for me at the front desk:

> Meet at Spanola, 15th Ave. S., to discuss
> your future. If any.

I changed my shirt and took Dolly's car to the Spanola, a Spanish restaurant in the music district, about a block from Lisle's office and within easy walking distance of the Country Music Hall of Fame and Museum.

The outside of the place was not promising. Somebody wanted it to look like a pink hacienda, but the phony adobe walls and artificial palm tree ruined the effect. A pair of floodlights bathed the front of the restaurant in garish light.

The inside was considerably better—dimly lit, with walls covered in deep crimson, brocaded wallpaper, and napkins matching in hue. Ornate crystal glassware stood on each table, and candles gleamed everywhere.

It was crowded with well-dressed diners. I recognized a few faces from the governor's party: Jerry Reed, looking like a visiting New Yorker in a light summer-weight suit; Jeannie C. Riley, dressed in a green cowboy vest and matching skirt, with a western hat of the same color slung around her neck.

Hilary was at a small table in the rear, sipping a Margarita. She had on a gray suit that was as severe as the way she bound up her hair in a tight golden knot . . . but there was no way of disguising the graceful curve of her long neck, nor the tantalizing contours of her petite body.

She saw me crossing the room, and the look she shot me was so chilly that her blue eyes might have been chiseled from ice.

"All right," I said, sitting down at her table, "I'm fired. Now let me explain—"

"Why, Gene!" Hilary purred in a too-sweet voice, "how nice of you to drop by! Are you sure I'm not imposing?"

"I'm sorry, but the reason I was late—"

"Let me guess. You forgot to set your watch back for Central Time, and you've been an hour late all week."

"I said I was sorry!"

"*And that's not good enough!*" Hilary snapped, regarding me as if I were some new form of repellent insect life. "All right," she said at last, "I *will* listen to your excuse. . . ."

"Good. The reason I was late—"

"—But it's not going to help, no matter what it is!"

I counted to five, then continued in as even a tone as I could muster. "The reason I was late is that Amanda Boulder's been murdered, and I was stuck at the police station."

Hilary started slightly, then stared at me with narrowed eyes to see whether or not I was lying. It took a long time for her to decide. "I have to admit," she finally said in an entirely different tone of voice, "that's one hell of an excuse."

The waiter loomed into view, and I ordered my usual Bushmill's on the rocks. Hilary put her elbows on the table and cupped her chin in her hands.

"All right," she told me. "Talk."

9

During dinner, I told Hilary all the details she wanted, including my personal impressions of the Boulders. It took a good two hours, and we lingered over coffee and liqueur to get it all in. Hilary was in cerebral ecstasy, and it must have frustrated her not to be able to write notes on the tablecloth.

At last she blotted her lips and, reaching for the check, suggested we get over to the Ramada so she could meet the Clan. She couldn't wait to start sleuthing.

But she had to contain herself a little longer because none of the Clan was at the motel. I called Charlie Lisle's office and got a late-working secretary who said that the Clan was having an emergency meeting at the manager's house. I secured the address and we drove there.

It was a one-story wooden ranch house some five miles north of town. Perched on top of a hill, the place had a columned front entrance with bright lights that showed the way to the carport. There was a red Plymouth Fury parked there, and the VW bus was standing right next to it. I pulled in on the other side of the Fury and braked to a stop.

Lisle himself opened the door. He saw us and frowned, but politely asked us in. I introduced Hilary to the family. Samson grunted a greeting but did not rise, while Brian merely inclined his head; neither of them looked especially happy. Pearl, on the other hand, got up, flashed a too-cheerful smile, and shook Hilary's hand. I suppose she decided it would be a good idea to make a positive first impression with the group's potential PR woman.

Dolly was seated off in a corner, a half-consumed drink in her hand. When she saw me, she smiled and patted the seat beside her. I crossed the room and sat down.

"Where's Josh?" I whispered.

"Said he had to stop off at the Opry. He'll be here soon."

Hilary was standing in the middle of the room looking over the scene. She turned to Lisle and said it was important she get the answers to some questions as quickly as possible.

"What kind of questions?" Lisle asked.

"About the murder."

Samson groaned. Lisle stared at Hilary with a blank expression, then said he didn't understand.

"Understand what?"

"We've been talking to the police for hours. Why should we go over the same ground with you?"

"Because if I can fill in the gaps, I can probably settle this whole business tonight." Hilary was certainly showing her customary lack of modesty; somebody snickered at the remark, and she cast an annoyed look in the direction of the sound.

Lisle wasn't having any. He patiently explained to Hilary that he had every confidence in the ability of the police to conduct the investigation. Hilary began to protest, but the manager held his ground.

"Miss Quayle," he enunciated precisely, "I'm afraid I must insist on my position." In his usual nervous fashion, his gaze focused on a spot a few inches to her left. "This is my home," he said, "and you're an uninvited guest in it. We have a welter of problems to discuss concerning Amanda Boulder's demise, and must solve them as quickly as possible. There is really no time for any other discussion." With that, he turned away from Hilary and began talking with the Boulders. She was clearly irked at being so abruptly dismissed, but as there was no alternative but for her to swallow it, she sat down on the opposite side of the room where she could watch everyone. But she avoided looking in my direction.

Samson was speaking, "Why the hell does it have to be one of the girls?"

"What do you suggest, Alvin?" Pearl drawled. "You want to dress up in long hair and a skirt?"

"If you don't get off my back, Pearl," he told her, "I'm liable to break yours!"

"Jee-zus!" she smirked, puckering her lips in a gross travesty of terror. "I'm *so* scared! Big bad Alvin's going to rough me up!"

Samson started to answer, but Dolly cut in and told them both to grow up. They subsided.

Lisle, who had been pacing, stopped in front of Samson. "I'm not saying you don't have the talent, Sam, but that's *not* a factor—I have to book the act, and I don't see getting dates without a Boulder girl singing the ballads."

"What makes you think *you'll* still be managing us?" Samson growled.

Lisle waved his hand impatiently. "Don't talk gibberish. Your act is not at a premium these days—"

"Who made it that way?" complained Pearl.

"—and you'd all have a hard time of it if you tried to get a different manager."

"You were ready enough to break us up," Dolly said quietly.

"That was different," said Lisle. "A simple case of good business, backing Amanda. Now that she's gone, it's a new story." He paused, spreading his hands in a gesture of surrender, "I just don't see any other way to go now—it's obvious that Dolly has to take the solo spot."

"*Dolly!*" Pearl shrieked, jumping to her feet. "You're out of your mind! What the hell does Miss Prancy Legs know about *singing?*"

"What the hell do *you* know about it?" Samson countered, but Pearl, ignoring him, repeated the question. Lisle refused to reply.

Over on the other side of the room, Brian was shaking his head and mumbling under his breath. Opposite him, Hilary sat and watched the family quarrel with unswerving interest.

Lisle asked Dolly if she would consider the solo spot. I'd observed her since he first made the suggestion. She was clutching her drink so tightly that her knuckles showed white against the glass. She tilted it back and drained the contents.

"Sure," she said, too casually, setting down the empty glass. "If you *really* want me to be the lead singer, I *guess* I could manage."

That was when the doorbell rang.

Opening the door, Lisle revealed a grinning Josh Mackenzie on the step, hands thrust deep in the pockets of his jeans. He ambled in, nodding to the group, started to speak, then noticed Hilary in the corner.

"I'm Josh," he told her, walking over to her chair and towering above her. "What's your name, sweetie?"

It was the wrong approach, but you couldn't blame him. Any other woman visiting Nashville at that time of year would have flipped over the personal attention. Hilary merely instructed him to take his belt buckle out of her range of vision. Josh stepped backward, startled at the rebuff.

I feel sorry for any dope who gets in Hilary's way, so I helped out Josh by formally introducing him to her. He mumbled an inept greeting, then hastily retreated to the bosom of his clan—or at least to that of Pearl.

"Josh," Lisle began, "we've been talking over the reformulation of the act. We have to settle tonight who will sing the ballad numbers. I feel there's no choice but Dolly."

"Why," whispered Dolly in my ear, "does Charlie make it sound like it's the last extremity?"

Josh shook his head. "Dolly's a picker, Charlie, and she pretends real good she can dance, but she's *not* a singer— you know that!"

"I can *too* sing!" she protested. "Gene here can tell you —can't you, Gene?" I nodded, embarrassed. Hilary stared at me with frank astonishment.

"Sure, sure, Dol, *maybe* you can sing a little." Dolly stared at him with a joyless smile that seemed to say, "Please don't do this to me. . . ."

The mute appeal went unheeded. Josh, still grinning, said, "Look, it doesn't matter whether Dolly thinks she can sing or not. It's already settled. Pearl here is gonna do the lead spot from now on." He gave the blonde a reassuring squeeze.

If Pearl were the least bit sensitive, she would have been uncomfortable, but she grinned at Josh in a way that I can only describe with a term I'd rather not use.

Samson started to protest, but Lisle beat him to it. "If you expect me to manage the Clan in the future, Josh, you're going to have to accord me the control I've lacked in the past. Pearl is *not* the best choice. She lacks expression. She has no hit songs to her credit. The public doesn't know her as well as they do Dolly who will attract attention on camera tomorrow night—"

"As a *dancer*," Josh reminded him.

"Yes," Lisle continued, "and that is *precisely* why she will go over so well. Everyone will wonder what kind of voice she has. She's been in the act for years, and everyone will be curious to hear Dolly's voice."

"There's only one thing wrong with your plan," Josh said, stretching his legs and leaning back in his chair.

"What?"

"I just had me a little talk with Harriet Marker and she did a quick sell job on the sponsor and the network. *They* want Pearl, not Dolly. The hit of the telecast will be poor bereaved Pearl Boulder singing 'I'll Never Call You Sweetheart Again' in memory of her deceased sister."

"*You goddamned crud!*"

We all whirled, stunned by the vehemence of the utterance. Brian Lucas, the same Brian who rarely said anything, was on his feet, his face livid with rage. "That does it!" he spat. "The whole of you are *filth!*" He would have added something further, but was too consumed with anger to speak. He whirled abruptly on his heel and, yanking open the front door, stormed out, slamming the door behind him.

The rest of the family stared at one another in disbelief. Then Samson rose, saying he'd better follow Brian and calm him down.

The rest of us sat quietly for a moment or two. Pearl

nestled her head against Josh's shoulder and whispered something in his ear. Dolly asked me to get her a refill, which I did. As I walked past Hilary on the way to the sideboard, she mumbled something about my talents as a butler, but I ignored her.

Following Brian's outburst, Lisle sat on the sofa and put his balding head in his hands, tuning out the rest of us. Josh got impatient and told Lisle he wanted an answer about Pearl as solo singer.

"Well," the manager replied sourly, "from what you've told me, I have no choice. It's Pearl, period—and I don't like it, Josh."

"Nobody said you had to," the other grinned. "You don't have to handle us, either. After tomorrow night, we'll have our pick of managers. Pearl will be hot property. Not that she's so bad *now*." He patted her and she giggled.

Just then, Samson reentered. "Brian," he announced, "is going to Tootsie's to get smashed—and so am I. We're taking the VW bus, in case anyone wants a ride." Josh said he had his own car, but would join them there.

"Who the hell wants you?" Samson retorted.

"Screw you, Alvin," said Pearl. "Josh and me'll find our own joint." She tugged Josh's arm and he rose. They left together.

"How about you?" Samson asked Dolly. "You coming?"

"No," she said rising unsteadily, "I'm supposed to check in at the police station and give them my statement. I think I'd better leave." She started toward the door, but was too unsteady to make it alone.

"You'd better let me drive," I said, taking her arm. I started to steer her out the door when a voice behind me made me stop.

"Would you mind very much," Hilary asked, "if I rode back with you, too, Gene?"

I started to apologize, but she waved me down impatiently. Standing on the doorstep, she turned to Lisle and said she wanted to know one thing.

"What *is* it?" he asked testily.

"Did Amanda Boulder really say she never wanted to sing 'I'll Never Call You Sweetheart Again' once she'd recorded it?"

"Yes," Lisle replied.

"Why?"

"It was too painful for her."

"But what made her change her mind?"

"Ask Josh," he said, closing the door gently, but firmly, in her face.

In her car, Dolly sat in the righthand front seat, saying nothing. I tried to engage her in conversation, but she confined her answers to monosyllables.

Only once did she open up. I said I thought the Clan acted a bit callous at the meeting.

"Why?"

"After all, Amanda *was* poisoned only this morning. Already everybody's ripping each other apart to replace her."

Dolly lightly rested a hand on my arm. "Gene," she said gently, "when you come from a family as big as mine, you get used to death. By the time I was ten, I had lost three brothers and a sister—two from malnutrition, one from fever, another was killed by a truck. You stop loving too much so it won't hurt so bad when you have to lose someone."

Just then, I realized we were being followed. The pair of headlights that had been coming and going in the rear-view mirror for the last several minutes had been niggling away at me subliminally. Now I pointed them out to Hilary.

"Uh–huh," she said drily, "nice work, Gene. You get an *F* for observation—they were there all the way *out* to Lisle's, too. . . ."

10

I decided not to shake our tail. For all I knew, it might have been set by Joe Cass, and then we'd only have the headache of proving that we didn't have anything to hide. On the outskirts of town, I braked for a traffic light. Dolly uttered an exclamation. Looking out the windshield, I saw an honor-system newspaper rack with late editions of *The Nashville Tennessean* in it. The story of Amanda's murder was splashed all over the front page.

"Oh, God," Dolly shuddered, "the price of fame. We won't go anywhere without being clawed at." She turned to me. "Gene, would you mind taking me to the motel so I can put on a pair of sunglasses? That, at least, will keep *some* of the vultures off my back."

"Sure," I said, detouring in the direction of the Ramada. Hilary and I waited in the Thunderbird while Dolly ran up to her room.

"Well preserved, isn't she?" Hilary asked. I didn't reply.

Dolly was gone several minutes. When she returned, she had a huge handbag slung over her shoulder, and was wearing a pair of dark glasses.

"Gene, honey," she said, getting back in the car, "there's no sense your hanging around the station house, it might take a long time. Can I call you when I'm through?"

"That'll be fine," I told Dolly. "Phone me at the motel."

"Better not," said Hilary in a tone I didn't like. "Gene-honey won't be there."

"Where am I going to be?" I asked politely.

"At Tootsie's."

"Okay." I looked at Dolly. "Can you page me there?"

"Yes," she hesitated, then added, "if it's all right with your employer? . . ."

I didn't answer that. Neither did Hilary. I put the car in drive and headed for the police station.

The station was only a few blocks from the Opry House. I pulled up at the curb, and Hilary told me to park because she wanted to meet Joe Cass.

The three of us walked in together, but Dolly immediately excused herself. Spotting a desk sergeant, she walked up to him and asked directions to the ladies' room. A pleased smile spread over his face when he realized who she was; he rose, pointed down a corridor, and watched as she disappeared through a doorway. He told us Cass was off duty and, after considerable urging from Hilary, reluctantly gave us the deputy's home number. We stepped into an alcove equipped with several pay telephones and I dialed Cass's number.

He wasn't thrilled to be disturbed. His wife had to fetch him from his cellar workshop, and he resented the interruption. "All afternoon," he complained, "the damn phone has been ringing. Reporters wanting to know if I'll make exclusive statements. Pressure from the commissioner who's getting it from the town council, which is being bothered by the governor. It's been a real ball!"

"Sorry to bother you, too, Joe," I said, "but I thought you'd want to know the Clan had an emergency caucus tonight. Pearl's been elected to take over Amanda's place in the act."

There was a brief silence on the other end, then Cass said, "Now that's interesting. Tell me about this get-together."

I outlined the meeting for him and, from time to time, he grunted to show he was listening. When I finished, Hilary nudged me, suggesting that I find out whether the poison had been identified as yet. I repeated the question, explaining it had been asked by my boss—who was going to wrap up his case in a neat little packet, probably overnight. He didn't seem overly impressed by the news.

"The poison's another goddamn headache!" he grumbled. "They've analyzed the contents of her stomach and the results are negative. No identification of any toxic substance. Not yet."

It was getting weirder by the minute. Amanda's mysterious poison seemed to have left no trace in the liquid that carried it nor in the body that received it. . . .

"*Now* what happens?" I asked Cass.

"The lab stays on it till they crack the thing. They've got to run a blind scan of the chemical constituents in the sample. It's probably going to take all night and then some."

"So at this point, the lab knows nothing?"

"Well," said Cass, "I wouldn't exactly say that. We *do* know that whatever killed Amanda isn't the garden-variety poison. We can rule out arsenic and strychnine, cyanide, and curare—all the better-known poisons. Whatever the substance was, it must be fairly exotic. That could eventually work in our favor. It could narrow down the list of candidates who might possess it."

"Uh–huh. Of course, knowing what it is still won't help—"

"Don't even mention how it was administered!" Cass snapped. "Look, it's getting late and I want to get back downstairs. If you think of anything else, give me a call . . . and don't mind if I bitch when you do."

I said okay and hung up. On the way to the car, I filled in the gaps for Hilary, who said nothing. Her lips were compressed in a thin, angry line, but I deigned not to notice her pique.

I began to soliloquize as I started the motor. "Let's see if I can figure out the agenda . . . first, Brian, who's now probably ripe to spill all the dirt about the Clan, considering his outburst. Then—"

"Why did you tell Cass that asinine business about how I was going to solve his case overnight? It made me sound like a goddamned *fool*."

I shrugged, but made no comment. We drove the few blocks to the Opry in silence, then pulled into the back lot of the auditorium. "That's Tootsie's over there," I said, pointing across the way. "Should I wait out here?"

She stared at me for a long time. "All right," she finally said, begrudgingly. "I'll try not to make any more cracks about older women."

"Fine," I said, shutting off the motor.

"—For tonight at least," she added, half to herself. I pretended not to hear.

11

Fog rolling in from the banks of the Cumberland choked the neon signs of Broadway with nimbuses of sickly light. On the other side of the wide main street, I could barely make out the steady stream of customers entering and leaving Ernest Tubb's Record Shop. In the endless array of shlock shops lining Fifth Avenue, coarse-set men in mail-order suits and women in cotton dresses queued up at the cash registers to buy such goodies as country-western magazines, wooden wall plaques emblazoned with sayings such as "We get too soon oldt and too late shmardt," and $1.98 "authentic" Gene Autry western guitars. I shuddered at a framed 3-D photograph in the window: It showed an actor wearing a crown of thorns, blood running down his forehead, and a look upon his face of mingled agony and beatitude. The picture shimmered and changed, and the eyes suddenly looked up longingly into the skies. Hilary grimly shook her head.

It was after ten o'clock. Tootsie's Orchid Lounge was filled to overflowing. Strategically situated near the Grand Ole Opry, Tootsie's is a magnet that attracts hundreds of thirsty country-music lovers: both young hopefuls fresh off the bus—their pockets stuffed with lyrics scrawled on lined tablet paper—and veteran sidemen and soloists ducking in for a quick shot between sets at the Opry.

There wasn't enough air space at the bar for a flea to breathe. Frowsy waitresses, their hair piled high, squeezed and shoved their way between shoulders to fill requests of the customers sitting in booths which lined the walls. The terrific din of voices was punctuated by the staccato stammer of a pinball machine and a jukebox's deafening blare as it blasted out "When I Get to Phoenix." After the song was over, a fierce-looking little woman of about fifty bounded around the side of the bar and fed coins to the music monster. Flickering, it sputtered, then made a fresh assault on my ears with "It Wasn't God Who Made Honky-Tonk Angels."

I spotted Samson sitting in one of the booths, his mouth encircling the neck of a Falstaff bottle. On the wall above, surrounded by a sea of ancient record-album covers, a photograph of Tex Ritter smiled down, as if to bless the libation ceremony in progress. Brian was nowhere in sight.

As we approached the table, the large man regarded us with bleary eyes, then, recognizing us, indicated the seat opposite and invited us to join him. We slid into the booth, and Samson bawled at one of the waitresses, who ignored him.

"Where's Brian?" I asked.

"In the back room. Goddamn reporters started in on us as soon as we sat down. Brian already had his belly full of talk about the act. He's off drinking by himself. *Hey, Bertha!*"

A frowning waitress with fat arms and iron-gray hair stomped over to the booth and told Samson to lower his voice. "Where the hell do you think you are?" she brayed belligerently. "You hush on up or Tootsie'll boot you out on your *ass!*"

"Just put a head on this," he said, shoving the bottle across the table.

"Hmph!" she snorted, "that's what people say when they use a *glass!*"

Samson made a rude sound. Hilary and I gave our drink orders, and Bertha departed to fill them.

"I hear you had quite a fight with Charlie Lisle," Hilary said. Samson looked at her sharply.

"Huh!" he grunted. "What he got is nothing compared to what I might have done. He's crossed me once too often."

"How?"

"*He* knows."

"Yes," said Hilary, "I'd like to know, too."

He shot her a glance which said, Are you always so damn nervy?, but decided to talk anyway. "Charlie promised to build me into a single act one of these days," Samson explained, "but every time, he turns around and helps one of my sisters, the little bastard."

"I suppose," Hilary suggested, "that Amanda's death didn't break you up all that much then."

"Hey!" he exclaimed, "what the hell is that? She was my sister!"

"Uh–huh. I've seen the kind of affection that binds your family together."

"Now look, don't go judging us on what you saw at Charlie's. Brian and me are pals and. . . ."

"What about you and Pearl?"

"Huh," he snorted, "she's a snot-nosed kid. Dumb, that's all."

"And Josh?" Hilary persisted. "I suppose the way he behaved with Pearl shows how deeply he felt for Amanda?"

Samson drained the bottle, banged the empty on the table and slumped back into the booth, fuzzy from drink. "Josh?" he repeated. "He's a big goddamn no-talent. The only reason he's still in the act—*Yo, Bertha! Don't run away!*"

"I told you to hush!" the waitress barked, grabbing the bottle as she hurried past. Suddenly, there was a murmur from the front of the room. I turned and saw Conway Twitty walking in. The little fierce-looking woman trotted out from behind the bar and punched buttons on the jukebox. The song playing rejected and one by Twitty started instead. There was applause, and the newcomer smiled in acknowledgment.

I turned back to Hilary and Samson. She was asking him why Josh and Dolly had split up. The big man, spreading his hands in a what-can-I-tell-you gesture, said he'd never found out the whole story. "But me and Brian know Josh was chasing other women. He's a professional stud!"

"How about Amanda? When did she start going with Josh?"

"Christ knows—*I* sure don't! When Merrill died, I—"

"Merrill?"

"Amanda's husband. Sweetest son of a bitch you'd ever hope to meet, couldn't do enough for her! That pair acted like teen-agers, holding hands, smiling at jokes that nobody else knew. When Merrill died, Amanda almost went out of her head. It happened on this picnic, which was *her* idea, so that afterward she blamed herself for Merrill's death. Christ! We had to put her in a hospital almost six months, we were that afraid she'd kill herself. Anyhow, what I'm trying to say is I figured after that, she'd *never* look at another man. . . ." Samson shook his head slowly. "See, this is what's so damned hard to figure—why would she turn around and want to marry *Josh* of all people?! I mean, *any* man would have been a surprise, but Amanda knew what a louse Josh is. It doesn't make sense! . . ."

"Maybe," I suggested, "we'll have a chance to find out pretty soon."

Hilary and Samson looked in the direction I indicated. Josh was at the bar, a shot glass in one hand, the back of the other hand up to his mouth. He was touching his tongue to it, and I guessed he'd sprinkled salt on it.

"When did he come in?" Hilary asked.

"*F* for observation," I retorted. "You should have noticed the lull."

I got a dirty look for that, but it was true. The hush had started at the front of Tootsie's and spread quickly through the rest of the place. Maybe it was motivated by respect for the supposedly grieved fiancé, though I suspected it was more a case of plain morbid curiosity.

A reporter approached Josh, and I saw the singer grin. He began talking to the journalist, and as he did, he licked the back of his hand every time he took a sip from his glass.

"What's he drinking?" I asked Samson. "Tequila?"

"Yep. He vacationed in South America once and picked up a taste for it."

"I wonder where Pearl is," Hilary mused.

I asked whether I should ask Josh to come over. Hilary nodded.

"In that case," said Samson, "you can count me out." He lurched to his feet and pushed over to the bar, yelling for another beer. The fierce-looking woman glared at him.

"What do you think?" I asked Hilary. "Was he as fond of Amanda as he says?"

She shrugged. "Can't say yet, insufficient evidence. Get Josh."

Prying the singer away from the Fourth Estate wasn't easy, but he finally slid into the booth, ordered an Oertel's chaser, and uncomfortably regarded Hilary. He still hadn't recovered from his initial rebuff.

"Okay, I'm here," he said. "What do you want, doll?"

I reminded him her name was Hilary, but she said he could call her Ms. Quayle. Josh hadn't been at Lisle's house when we arrived, so I had to explain how Hilary was trying to gather information on the murder.

"What do you want from me?" he asked unenthusiastically.

"The answers to a few questions."

"Such as?"

"Such as why Amanda sang 'I'll Never Call You Sweetheart Again' with new words."

"Hell, anybody can figure that out," Josh said belligerently. "She wanted to let everybody know how crazy she was for me."

"Charlie Lisle claimed she never wanted to sing it again," I said.

"She changed her mind," Josh replied, perhaps a little too casually. It was the only comment he would make about it.

"Why did you and Dolly get a divorce?" Hilary asked abruptly.

It startled him and he showed it. "What the hell business is it of yours?" he demanded.

"I heard she left you because you were running around with other women." That was stretching it a little, but I figured she was on a fishing expedition. It worked.

"What do you mean she left me?" Josh demanded. "Who the hell told you that? It was the other way around!"

"Oh, *really?*" Hilary asked ironically.

"Yeah—really! Everybody thinks Dolly's the cutest little piece in Nashville—well, *believe me,* she's not so cute once you live with her." He jabbed a finger in my direction. "If she once gets her hooks into you, you'd better lock up the checkbook. She'll sign *your* name so fast—anytime she thinks she needs a new costume!" He glanced at his watch and rose. "Look, I'm gonna fetch Pearl; she had to stop off at the dressing room. You got any more questions for me?"

"They can wait," said Hilary, "if you're bringing her over here."

"I guess I could," he said unenthusiastically. "But it better not take too much longer."

"We'll be here when you get back," Hilary said. Josh left and we sat for a while. One of the waitresses called my name and I went to the phone. It was Dolly. She was finished at the police station and wanted me to pick her up. I said I'd drive over right away.

Hilary had to wait for Josh and Pearl, but I told her I'd come right back once I'd dropped off Dolly at the motel.

I walked out and turned toward Fifth Avenue. The city was now completely cloaked in the dank mist rising from the river. I reached the corner when a racket behind me made me turn around. I saw Samson propelled through the front entrance of Tootsie's with considerable force. The fierce little woman I'd seen tending bar was right behind him, shouting, "Don't show your face in here again tonight."

The giant could have squashed her with one blow of his massive fist, but he confronted her instead like a wayward schoolboy and pleaded in a wheedling tone of voice: "Aww, let me come back in. I didn't mean to get so loud!"

"Go on home and go to bed," she growled, then stamped

inside, slamming the door behind her. Samson stood looking at the door, his hands clenching and unclenching, but he didn't follow her inside. He was standing there when I turned the corner and began to walk toward the car.

12

On the way to the police station, I drove a couple of blocks out of the way just to see whether someone was still following the Thunderbird. The headlights were there again. Chances were that it was a police tail, and I marveled that Joe Cass could spare so many patrols—for if we were being shadowed, then it was a cinch that all the Boulders were. I figured Cass wouldn't have many men to spare, what with the awards ceremony drawing thousands of tourists to the Greater Nashville area.

I pulled up to the station house. Dolly was waiting for me on the steps, and when I saw what she looked like, I jumped out of the car and ran around to open the door for her. She was exhausted, physically and emotionally, and practically collapsed against my shoulder. I steadied her; she rested her head against my chest.

"Thank you for being here," she whispered, squeezing my hand. I cradled her head as she sobbed quietly. It took a long time before she calmed down.

It was almost 1:00 A.M. when I returned for Hilary. She

was waiting in front of Tootsie's. "Where the hell have you been?" she demanded. "I was just getting ready to call a cab!"

"I'm sorry," I began, "but Dolly wasn't feeling well and. . . ."

"My dear Gene," she said, too sweetly, "maybe you'd better remember that Dolly Boulder does *not* pay your salary. . . ."

"Don't start up with me, Hilary! Dolly was in bad shape."

"*Ha!*"

"Listen to me—she was nearly hysterical. I couldn't leave her alone."

"I'll just bet you couldn't!"

Quietly I warned her to cut it out, but she paid no attention.

"The *least* you could have done was phone and let me know you were going to be late!"

"I *told* you I was sorry, Hilary! I lost track of the time."

"Yes. I suppose you were too preoccupied to glance at your watch."

I lost my temper and said I was sick of her innuendos and petty bitchiness. I told her she had so little human warmth that she couldn't even comprehend the quality in someone else. I accused her of trying to turn a personal tragedy into an intellectual game for her own kicks. I was frankly astonished at my own vehemence. Okay, I said to myself as I wound down, you've got it all out of your system. Now it's pink slip time.

But Hilary didn't counterattack. She just stood there, white-faced, lips trembling, looking like a child who had been spanked without cause. Then she mastered her emotions and regarded me frostily.

"Drive me back to the motel," she ordered, marching off to the Opry parking lot.

The deep-freeze continued during the ride back to the motel. I already regretted my outburst and tried to bridge the communications gap by asking whether Josh had told her anything else, or if she'd had a chance to question Pearl.

"They didn't come back," she said curtly. There was no more talk during that ride.

As soon as I parked, Hilary started off for her balcony-level room. I followed her.

"Why the hell are you trailing along?" she demanded, rounding on me.

"It's late," I said. "I intend to walk you to the door of your room."

"Suit yourself, Galahad." She started off again, neither welcoming nor forbidding my company. I might have been a gnat for all the notice she took of me.

As she approached the angle of the corridor where her room was located, Hilary sarcastically addressed me over her shoulder. "All right," she said, "the bitch is home safely —nobody is going to spring out of the shadows and attack her. *Now get lost!*"

Just then, we heard a man cough. It was Brian. The paunchy bass player looked the worse for drink, and a deep frown pulled the corners of his mouth down; his hands were jammed in his pockets, and his head drooped on his chest. He'd been leaning against Hilary's door, but straightened when he saw us.

"Would you mind moving?" Hilary snapped. "I want to go to bed."

"Hold on a minute," he said, curiously tense. "Can I ask you something?"

Hilary shrugged. "Ask. I don't have to answer."

"Is it true what you said about figuring out who killed my cousin Amanda?"

"*Me?*" Hilary asked sarcastically, tossing me a poisonous glance. "You don't think *I* would interfere in your family's personal tragedy, do you? It's none of *my* business!"

He regarded her intently, trying to reach a decision. "Well," he said finally, "if you *should* decide to make it your business, I'll tell you anything you need to know."

"Why?" she asked. "What's it mean to you?"

He fidgeted, shifting from foot to foot. "It's like this," he explained. "When I was a kid, my mom and dad died, and the Boulders took me in. Ma Boulder was so busy with her own kids she didn't have time to give me much extra attention . . . and I really needed it, being an orphan and all. It was Amanda who . . . how can I tell you . . . *really* became a mother to me. . . ." He paused, waiting for her to reply.

"Very unconvincing," she said, taking out the key to her room. "Now move out of the way."

"It's the truth!" he exclaimed. "Amanda meant the whole world to me!"

"Good night," she said, shoving him aside and unlocking her door.

Brian stuck out his foot and held the door open. I got behind him, ready to apply pressure in case he meant to get rough. But he just stood there, cursing under his breath, finally saying, "All right! You want the *real* reason? I want to get even with those miserable bastards—and if it means dragging out all the dirty family laundry, then I'll be tickled to do it!

"You know how many years I've been in the act? *Nine,*" he complained. "Nobody pays any mind to me; it's always 'good old Brian, he never says nothing cause he never has nothing to say.' None of them ever thinks, 'Hey, maybe old Brian knows how to sing, too. Maybe we should give him a chance to do a spot, a little number, one of these days'—instead of just sticking me in the back slapping bass and forgetting I exist!"

By the end of his tirade, Brian was huffing and puffing to catch his breath. Hilary regarded the musician for a moment with sour amusement, then opened the door to her room and told him to come in.

When I tried to follow, she slammed the door in my face.

13

I got back to my room at 1:30, too worked up to go to bed. There was the usual writing desk with motel stationery in the room. I sat down at it and began to itemize the tangle of problems my mind was trying to sort. On one side of a sheet of paper, I wrote the names of the Clan, including Charlie Lisle's; on the other side, I left spaces for possible motives. I repeated the procedure for means and opportunity.

Tackling the motive sheet first, I realized the girls had the strongest reasons for wanting Amanda out of the way, at least if Joe Cass was correct in saying they'd kill for the star spot on the telecast. But the men couldn't be eliminated on that score either. The only person I couldn't assign a motive for killing Amanda was Charlie Lisle; he had every reason to want her alive and well.

If the motive sheet suggested little, the other two lists were even less helpful. "Means" was a total blank, since the lab hadn't yet analyzed what kind of poison she'd swallowed, and "opportunity" could hardly be discussed until means had been settled. But even if the toxin were quick-acting and needed only to be ingested to take effect, the Clan and I had eaten lunch together; it would be most unlikely that the murderer could have administered the poison with so many people watching. I suddenly realized that Cass and I were assuming that Amanda had swallowed the poison—when perhaps it had been administered subcutaneously. Might the killer have bumped Amanda "by accident" and delivered a fatal pinprick? I didn't like the idea: It sounded like a scene from a spy thriller. Still, I supposed, it had better be explored. It was the only theory so far that might account for the absence of poison in the glass and pitcher.

I remembered the press clippings that Cass had let me copy. Opening the file, I began reading through the clips. There were a lot, but few had much to disclose about the family. The background on how Pappy Boulder founded the Clan was told in several articles, but then I already knew about that. Several clips told about Amanda coming back into the family act after dropping out of public life following her husband's death. The details of the latter were in the file, too, and they substantiated what Samson said—the Clan was out on a picnic when Merrill Gannett stepped on an insect, suffered an allergic reaction, and died.

However, there was one new fact I uncovered that surprised me. I'd assumed that Pappy Boulder had died a natural death, since he was ninety years old when he succumbed, but I was wrong. He was in a car crash on Route 66 while the family was on its way to sing at a barn dance. The clipping was short and gave no details of the accident. I wondered who'd been driving.

The phone rang. It was almost 2:30, a hell of a time for anyone to be calling. I thought it might be Hilary, but it turned out to be Dolly. I could barely hear her. She was whispering and sounded frightened.

"Gene," she begged, "would you come over to my room? I know it's late, but—" she hesitated, "I'm scared."

I told her I'd be right over, hung up, and threw on some clothes. Dolly was wearing a negligee when I arrived. She gave me a grateful hug and asked me in.

Lines of worry crinkled her forehead, yet she still looked young enough to be my kid sister. I sat on the edge of the bed beside her and asked what was wrong. Reaching over to the night table, Dolly picked up a small square of notepaper, explaining that she'd been asleep when the phone rang, waking her.

"I heard somebody breathing on the other end and thought it was some pervert who found out where I was staying. I started to cuss him out but then he—she—spoke."

"He? She? Which was it?"

"I couldn't tell. It was weird . . . whoever it was had to be disguising his—her voice. Anyway, the caller said, 'Look under your door,' then hung up."

"So you were meant to see the note right away," I said, pointing to the slip of paper.

"Uh–huh. It was under the door. Here—take a look at it. . . ."

She held the paper out. I took it and opened it up. The handwriting, a childlike scrawl, was in pencil. It read:

> *Old City Cemetery—now.*
> *Urgent.*
> *Rawlings Sanders.*

"Do you know anybody by that name?" I asked. The question seemed to amuse Dolly.

"Silly!" She laughed. "Rawlings Sanders didn't write the note; it's the name on a tombstone! You Yankees don't know anything!" She grew serious once more. "Whoever wrote this must want me to meet him at the Sanders monument."

"*Whoever* wrote this?" I echoed, amazed. "You must recognize the handwriting!"

She shook her head. "I don't. Do you?"

"No, *I* don't, but you can't look me in the eye and say *you* don't know who wrote this!"

"But I'm telling you I *don't* know!"

"It doesn't make sense! Nobody would expect you to respond to a wild request like this unless he was pretty sure you'd know who sent the message."

Dolly studied her hands and avoided meeting my gaze. "I . . . I'm not sure," she said after a brief silence. "I don't want to say until I'm positive. . . ."

"All right, then . . . but what do you want *me* to do?"

"Please come with me, Gene," she said, putting a hand on my arm. "I'm scared to go there alone."

I couldn't believe it. "Are you nuts, Dolly? You're not really thinking of obeying this thing, are you? You're liable to end up like Amanda!"

"I *know* it's dangerous, but I have to go! If I can find out who killed my sister! . . ."

"It's insane! You'd better turn this note over to the police!"

"*No! I won't!*" She stopped, a sudden hardness appearing in her eyes. But Dolly was instantly contrite. "I'm sorry, Gene, I'm just very upset, *you* understand."

I nodded. She looked into my eyes, raised a hand to my cheek and gently caressed it. "Please," she pleaded, "*please* go with me. . . ."

I tried to say no, but Dolly's delicate lips framed the word "please" again.

"All right," I murmured, "I'll come with you."

She whispered, "Thank you," as our lips came close together, and met. It was a long time before we ended our embrace.

14

Dolly put on a lacy white blouse and a pair of black satin pants that I couldn't take my eyes off. She slung a bag over her arm and was ready.

I got behind the wheel, wondering what the hell to do about our tail. Should I shake it? But if it were the police, they'd know I'd done it deliberately, and that might cause complications later. On the other hand, it wasn't going to look too cute to them, either, leading them to the gates of a graveyard. I ended up doing nothing. If the cops decided to horn in on our nocturnal expedition, Dolly would simply have to show them the note, that's all there was to it.

I parked the Thunderbird on Fourth Avenue South and followed Dolly to the cemetery's main entrance on Oak Street. The night was chilly and river fog still clung to the ground. Dolly had brought a sweater with her, which was smart. As we stopped in front of the low iron gates of the cemetery, she wrapped the garment around her shoulders.

Though the gates were locked, they weren't high and the iron fence on either side of the massive stone pillars in which the gates were set looked easy to climb.

"Do you think we could shinny over that?" Dolly asked, pointing to the fence. I nodded. She walked over to it, telling me to give her a boost, and I did. A few seconds later, we were both standing inside the cemetery. Dolly clasped my hand and drew me close. I could feel her shivering.

A wide central path stretched arrow-straight into the depths of the graveyard; it was lit by street lamps that shone feebly in the mist. The scene reminded me of the sinister Avenue of the Dead in Middle Eastern fantasies.

We walked down the broad main thoroughfare, hand in hand. It ran about five hundred feet before it reached a circular parking lot in front of a massive central administration building that loomed ominously out of the fog. There was no breeze at all, and the only sounds disturbing the stillness were footsteps and the sibilant whisper of our breath.

"That's where we're going," Dolly said, pointing to the right. "The Ann Rawlings Sanders grave is just off the circle, practically next to the flagpole."

"Who was she?"

"She was a girl who used to meet her lover on a bluff overlooking the Cumberland. The two of them got into a lovers' quarrel, and she leaped into the river and died. You'll see the rock she jumped from: They used it for her tombstone."

We continued to walk. When we reached the parking circle, Dolly tugged me gently and I followed her around the right-hand perimeter of the curve. I saw a massive unhewn gravestone in the distance and asked Dolly if that was it.

"Yes," she replied, "but I don't see anybody waiting for me."

"Neither do I." In spite of the fog, visibility was somewhat better at the grave because floodlights were trained up on the stone, bathing the area in a frozen mortuary glare.

On top of the monument a metal frame that looked a little like a pagoda had been mounted. In it was suspended a wrought-iron lantern.

"The lamp," said Dolly, "was put there by Ann's lover because she'd always been afraid of the dark. They used to light it every night and extinguish it in the morning, but now they use spotlights. I don't think that's nearly as nice. . . ."

She leaned against a nearby tree trunk. I stood next to her, bracing palm-flat against the bole with one hand. A cricket shrilled, then was still. We waited a long while. The only noises were the suspiration of our breath and the occasional muted rumble of a distant vehicle. At last, Dolly looked in my eyes. She smiled.

"Hi," she said.

"Hi."

We looked at each other for a moment, and then we kissed.

"I guess," said Dolly, a long time later, "nobody is going to show up."

"The fact that I'm here may be keeping them off."

"Uh–huh. I thought of that."

"Well, what do you think? Should we go back to the motel? You've got a busy day ahead of you."

"Give it another ten minutes," said Dolly, looking at her watch.

"Okay. While we're waiting, let's talk."

"About what?" she asked. I hesitated. Dolly looked at me quizzically. She touched my cheek gently with the tips of her fingers. "What about, Gene?" she whispered.

"About you and Josh."

Her delicate caress became a brittle touch.

"Why did you split up?"

"Why does anything come to an end?" she asked. The warmth had left her voice. "One day you're in love, the next day everything is bleak, dead—who knows why?" She turned away. I saw her begin to tremble. Opening her purse, Dolly rummaged inside, withdrew a hip flask half-full of amber liquid. She unscrewed the top, gestured with the bottle and raised it to her lips. "I snitched it," she confided, then took a small sip and passed it to me. I never got my hands on it. Dolly's eyes suddenly widened and a look of horror appeared in them. She snatched away the flask and began to back off.

"Dolly, what's the matter?"

"Don't come near!" she said in a choked voice, then whirled and swung the flask against a gravestone with all her might. Splinters flew in every direction, yet she continued to dash the bottle against the marker until there was nothing left but the jagged neck, which she ground against the granite, pulverizing the glass.

"Dolly!" I yelled. *"What's wrong?"*

The last shard fell from her fingers, and she dropped to her knees. Slipping off a shoe, she began pounding the larger fragments of glass into powder. She cut herself several times and her wrist and fingers grew wet with blood.

I grabbed her by the shoulders and pulled her to her feet. She threw her arms around me and clung as tightly as she could, sobbing. She shook uncontrollably.

"Gene," she cried, "the liquor—it's burning my throat. . . ." Then she started to gasp for breath.

I picked up Dolly in my arms, and she clutched my shirt so tightly that it pinched. Her bloody fingers made a crimson smear on the cloth.

Dolly's body was feather light. I carried her as quickly as I could, staggering back down the Avenue of the Dead toward the main entrance. She hung limp and lifeless in my arms. . . .

"*Halt!*"

As I reached the gate, two figures suddenly appeared out of the fog and blocked my path. I found myself standing face to face with a pair of uniformed patrolmen.

15

I could have kissed them both.

"Quick!" I gasped, "we've got to get her to a hospital! She's been poisoned!"

I carried Dolly to the patrol wagon and one of the cops opened up the door for me. I handed the other the keys to the Thunderbird and a few seconds later, both cars headed off for Nashville General.

They took her to the emergency room. In other circumstances, the usual red tape might have held us up, but the combined facts that it was a police escort and that the patient was Dolly Boulder got the hospital staff hopping; I answered the questions while they put Dolly on a table and wheeled her out.

A few minutes later, Joe Cass arrived. His eyes were heavy with interrupted sleep, while his hair was a rumpled mess. The deputy was in no mood to be friendly. "What in holy hell were you doing breaking into that cemetery in the middle of the night?" he demanded.

I outlined the events of the evening for him. The look of disbelief grew upon his face as I talked, but I really couldn't blame him. I probably wouldn't have bought it, either, if I were he.

"That's a pip of a story!" he said when I was finished. Turning to one of the patrolmen who had escorted Dolly to the emergency room, Cass ordered him back to the graveyard to verify the business about the bottle.

"Get whatever you can in the way of splinters. Have the lab run a check on prints," Cass told the cop, who left at little less than a run.

Cass regarded me sourly. "The chances of getting a usable print are about zilch," he grumbled. "Why the hell would she want to go and smash it? It's crazy!"

"Not if she were trying to protect somebody."

"Yeah," he said. "For all I know, you were the one who really knocked it apart."

"*Me?*"

"You come running out of the cemetery with a sick girl in your arms. You say she swallowed poison, then broke the bottle so nobody could identify its owner. We've only got your word for it. . . ."

"Look, Joe—don't make things so complicated. I knew damn well you were tailing us. Would I try anything stupid?"

"You *might,* figuring we'd have to believe your story, since it'd be too wild for anyone to invent and imagine he could get away with."

I waved a deprecating hand at him. "Joe, you're just pissed because they hauled you out of bed. Why don't you check on the note? That'll confirm my story."

"Yeah, I've got a man over at the motel looking for it."

"It's not at the motel! I saw Dolly put it in her bag while we were riding over in the car."

"Well, it's not there now."

"*What?*"

"Either everything you're telling me is a bunch of crap, or else Dolly wanted to make absolutely certain that nobody would know who was after her. There was no note in her bag."

Cass was sitting on a wooden bench beneath a large circular clock that read 4:15. I got up and began to pace.

"Maybe if you can get me writing samples of the rest of the Clan's handwriting," I said, "I could identify who wrote the note—I can still see it pretty clearly in my mind."

"Uh–huh," Cass said unenthusiastically. "And another thing about this note story—"

"*Now* what?"

"We've had every one of you under observation. If somebody slipped that note under Dolly's door, he must have been invisible."

"You've kept tabs on all the Boulders and—?"

"*And*—except for Pearl—they all were either in their rooms since two o'clock, or are otherwise accounted for."

I asked him to run it down for me, which he did. *Josh* left Tootsie's to get Pearl at the Opry, let himself in with a key through the back door of the Ryman, stayed for fifteen minutes, left alone; he drove back to the Ramada, went to his room, hadn't been seen since. *Brian*, observed waiting outside Hilary's room, later returned to his own room. *Samson* hit several bars after Tootsie's, finally sacking out in the VW bus. *Pearl* was missing. She was seen entering the Opry, but not leaving it. Cass admitted she might have got out another way without his man knowing.

A phone call for Cass came as he was finishing off the catalog of the Clan's whereabouts. He listened for a few seconds, then hung up.

"Okay," he said, "they found the glass like you said—smashed to hell except for one or two chips that *might* be big enough to get a couple of prints from."

"So you're starting to believe me?"

"Who said?" Cass grunted. "It's easier to give you the benefit of the doubt. For now."

Two minutes later, the other cop called in to say that the note in the strange handwriting was not in Dolly's bedroom. I could have told him that without looking.

"Can you make a guess," the deputy asked, "who Dolly is protecting?"

I shook my head. "She's fiercely loyal to the Clan, but there's a limit to how far a person will turn the other cheek. It doesn't make sense." I held up a finger to make a point. "Now that I think of it, Joe, we can't even really assume that Dolly was the intended victim. She said she 'snitched' the flask. Maybe it was meant for someone else, but she drank it by accident. . . ."

"Okay," said the policeman, "but how about that note? If that wasn't a *lure*, what is? Who wrote it? What was the reasoning behind it—assuming that there really *was* a note." I began to protest but he gestured impatiently. "The worst thing about it, Gene, is that there's no way it could have been slipped under her door. She would have seen it when she entered the room. Afterward nobody was observed near the door until the time *you* showed up. Now, go figure *that* out!"

I couldn't. We not only had a poison that left no trace, but also a mysterious note-writer who apparently could become invisible at will.

"Have you gotten any results," I asked, "on the nature of the poison?"

He shook his head. "It's a real bitch—we had to send a specimen out to a lab upstate: They've got a computer that's supposed to be able to read out just about any toxin. All we can do is wait."

"How long?"

"Today. Tomorrow. When it comes, it comes."

Cass's philosophy was no help in coping with Dolly's illness. Every passing orderly got the third degree from me, but none of them knew how she was doing. At last, I decided I might just as well wait in ignorance at the motel as at the hospital. I left the phone number with the night nurse in case she received news of Dolly's condition within the next few hours.

It was 5:30 when I got into the Thunderbird and drove back to the Ramada. I didn't return to my room. I hated to admit it, but I needed Hilary's help.

I pounded on her door for several minutes before I could rouse her. When she heard it was me, she cursed and told me to beat it, but I stood my ground and eventually she opened the door.

A stream of invective greeted me at first, but then she saw me and faltered. "What in hell happened to you?" she asked. "You look awful!"

"Can I come in?"

She nodded and opened the door. The room was dark, and Hilary was wearing nothing but a short, see-through negligee, all rose lace and silk. "I don't have a robe," she said, "so you'll have to pardon how I look. You've seen women before."

I was too tired to pay more than passing notice. I started in on the events of the evening, omitting no detail. When I was finished, she sat quietly on the edge of the bed, regarding me curiously.

"What do you want from me?" she asked.

"If Dolly pulls out of this, there's liable to be another attempt on her life. If she doesn't, I want whoever did it."

"Let me get this straight: You're asking *me* to meddle in the Clan's private tragedies? Aren't you afraid I'll turn everything into a big intellectual game?"

"Hilary," I said earnestly, resting my hands on her shoulders, "I feel rotten for what I said last night. I was an S.O.B., I admit it."

"Please don't touch me," she said, looking at my hands on her shoulders. Hilary rose, walked to the dresser, squeezing the knuckles of one hand in the other.

"All right," she said, avoiding my eyes. "It's obvious you care enough about her to swallow your pride. I'll try not to take advantage. Now the first thing we need to know is where Dolly got the hip flask. Next, where's Pearl? Third, bring me the press clippings."

"What about Brian?" I asked. "Did he have anything valuable to tell you last night?"

"Oh, not much," Hilary drawled, "only that Josh and Pearl have been bedmates for months. That Amanda spent six months in a rest home after her husband died. She tried to kill herself, used to have hysterics if anybody even said the word 'picnic' in front of her. What else? Charlie Lisle is gay, hates women, wants Samson's body. Samson never says yes—or no. Josh walked out on Dolly because she used to make him punch a time clock—which is the third answer I've gotten to *that* question. Finally, Brian thinks Amanda was going to marry Josh out of spite."

"Spite?"

"He overheard Josh telling Amanda that before he died, Merrill Gannett was screwing his sister-in-law Dolly. Pardon the bluntness: That's the way Josh put it. Other than those tidbits," Hilary added dryly, "Brian didn't have too much to say. . . ."

16

Saturday morning saw the vultures descend.

Charlie Lisle would have been willing to bow out of the press conference at the Highway Shack Motel, but Hilary talked to him and got permission to handle it herself. She also phoned Cass and discussed her strategy with him. After she hung up, she told me the deputy reluctantly agreed to let us release the details of the poisoning.

"When the papers stress the impossible crime," she said, "it might give the murderer a sense of false security—enough so for him to make some kind of mistake."

There were plenty of other celebrities in the private dining room where the conference was held: Sonny James, Buck Owen, Minnie Pearl, Judy Lynn, Jerry Lee Lewis, and several more, but the Boulder Clan ranked highest in importance in the eyes of the press.

It wasn't a formal speech-making gathering, but a buffet brunch with journalists and performers eating together at a series of circular dining tables. Reporters took potluck with whichever celebrity happened to be sitting at his table, but a steady stream of writers flowed in our direction.

Hilary explained the story of Amanda's untraceable poison, as well as the calamity that befell Dolly in Old City Cemetery.

Charlie Lisle sat beside her, looking thoroughly miserable; he didn't say two words the whole morning. Samson and Brian were there, too, both of them the worse for wear. Josh sat across from me. He was unusually subdued, and he replied to all questions politely but without his customary enthusiasm. One reporter asked him where Pearl was, and he shrugged.

"Guess she must have slept late."

Actually, no one knew where the blonde was. She hadn't slept in her room the night before. The last person to see her was Josh, when he dropped her off at the Ryman.

A reporter from *GRIT* approached the table. He was holding an autograph book. I'd met him Thursday night at the governor's mansion. He stepped up to Samson, saying he'd promised a niece he would get the signatures of as many celebrities as possible. Samson nodded wearily and asked how he'd like it inscribed, signing the way he was told. He then passed the book along to Brian, who did the same, passing it in turn to Josh.

"Has anybody heard how Dolly's doing?" the reporter asked.

"Yes," said Hilary, "she's out of danger, probably because she only took a sip of the drink. Amanda swallowed a glassful."

That news pleased me, of course. I'd already been over to the hospital that morning, but wasn't admitted to her room. However, I'd been assured she probably would be released later that afternoon.

A *Time* feature writer sat down and asked Josh to describe his feelings on learning his fiancée had been poisoned. It was the tenth time the question had been asked that morning. I slipped out of my seat and crossed the room to a table in a far corner.

"Nice work," I told Harry MacArthur, the *GRIT* reporter. "I appreciate the help."

"No sweat," he replied, "just give me an exclusive when the story's ready to break." He pushed the autograph book across the table to me.

While I examined the signatures, MacArthur said, "I think I know how that poison trick might have been worked."

I looked at him quizzically. MacArthur, a plodding middle-aged man with lifeless gray hair on a massive skull, seemed the least likely source for an answer to the poisoning problem. But I encouraged him to speak.

"It's farfetched," he demurred, smiling. "In fact, I can't even remember what the stuff was called, but we ran a piece in *GRIT* some time ago about a poison—"

"An unusual substance?"

"Yeah. If it's as rare as I remember it being, it'd be pretty tough to figure out how the killer got hold of it in the first place."

"What's the name of this drug?"

"I forget. It had a nickname—what the hell was it? I'll try to remember. Anyhow, the funny thing about it was that it allows a killer to poison his victim days or even *weeks* before the drug takes effect. . . ."

Curiouser and curiouser. I told MacArthur his mystery drug sounded pretty exotic.

"Uh–huh. That's why we ran the story in our 'Odd, Strange and Curious' column. Look, I have to call Williamsport later today. I'll ask them to find the story and read it over the phone. I'll make you a copy. Where shall I leave it?"

I gave him the room number at the Ramada. He jotted it down, then rose, shook hands, and began to head for another table and its resident cluster of luminaries. But MacArthur stopped and returned to me. "I remember the nickname," he said.

"What is it?"

He smiled wryly. "You're gonna love it—shades of Abraham Merritt and Sax Rohmer. It's called 'the devil's timeclock'. . . ."

He waved cheerfully and walked off.

17

Hilary and Lisle rode over to the hospital with me to get Dolly. We stopped off first at the Opry on the manager's request, and he ran inside while we waited. He was back in less than ten minutes and had an air of grim satisfaction.

Dolly was in the lobby when we arrived, pale but smiling. Her hair was matted, and her eyes were red from lack of sleep, but she still looked lovely. I walked over and embraced her.

"Not here, Gene!" she smiled, jerking her head at the others. "I embarrass easily!" But she gave me a quick kiss just the same.

Her hands were swathed in bandages, and, as she held them up for Charlie Lisle to see, she smiled ruefully.

"I guess," said Dolly, "I won't be much good tonight. I don't think I'll be able to pick mandolin again for a few days, Charlie."

"That's all right," the manager assured her. "You won't have to. You're singing solo tonight!"

I thought she'd faint. Her legs went wobbly and I had to grab her arm to lend support.

"You're kidding, Charlie! Don't be cruel!"

"I'm *not*. Thanks to your scrape with death, you are now hot news, a lot hotter than Pearl. I just had a talk with the agency and network people, and they said to give you the ballad number."

"Oh, my God!" she exclaimed, panicking. "What am I going to sing? I don't have any gown to wear!"

"We'll fix up something," Lisle replied, "don't worry about it. You'll do Amanda's number. It's got built-in appeal; Josh was right about *that*. . . ."

"But look at me!" Dolly wailed, holding up her bandaged hands. "I can't play!"

"You don't need to. Just hold those hands up to the camera like you're doing, and every heart in the country will go out to you," Lisle said.

The word had reached the press that Dolly was going to be discharged. When we came out of the hospital, she was suddenly surrounded by cameramen and reporters. I'd expected such a scene, of course, but I was surprised by the spontaneous cheer she got. Dolly's ordeal had endeared her to the press. When she saw the reception waiting for her outside, Dolly smiled uncertainly. I gave her arm a quick squeeze and whispered, "Don't be afraid, you've earned it." She wrinkled up her nose at me, then faced the press with a merry smile on her lips.

"Now, come on," she laughed, "don't photograph me like this! My hair's a mess, and I look horrible!"

At least five cameramen assured her that she was the epitome of feminine beauty, and she thanked them before turning to answer the questions of an AP correspondent. It took us twenty minutes to get away from there. By that time, Dolly looked positively radiant. But Hilary was not enjoying it, and I began to worry that she might make herself obnoxious again. My fears were justified. As we drove off, she turned to Dolly and asked if she would mind answering a question.

"Not at all. What is it?"

"I'd like to know," said Hilary, "whether you ever had an affair with Merrill Gannett?"

The atmosphere changed so fast it nearly gave me the bends. I shot Hilary an angry glance, then looked at Dolly in the rear-view mirror. Her face was positively white.

"How *dare* you suggest that?" she demanded. "Merrill's been dead for over two years. He was a wonderful man— and he loved my sister!"

"Yes, I'm sure he did," Hilary said sweetly, "but that's not who I asked about."

Dolly said something to her I never would have expected to hear from her mouth, but I didn't blame her in the least. Then she asked how I could stand working for a woman like Hilary.

"Sometimes," I replied, "I wonder about that. . . ."

I parked in the Opry lot. Dolly had to get started right away on her number for that night's broadcast. Lisle wanted to talk to the rest of the Clan.

Inside, Samson greeted Dolly cordially. Josh waved at her in nonchalant fashion, but she ran up to him and gave him a hug.

"Okay, Dolly," Lisle remarked, "you've got a heavy day ahead of you. Go try on some of Amanda's gowns, see if they'll fit you."

"Okay," she said. "You wait here, I'll be right back."

When she was gone, Lisle asked me to get Brian. I walked over to the men's dressing room and found him tuning up his bass. I said the manager needed to see him right away, and he accompanied me to the backstage corridor where the other men waited.

Lisle nodded at Brian, then said, "Gentlemen, we've got a real problem with the group slot for tonight. If we can't find Pearl, we're going to have to give up the air time."

"Christ," Josh spat, "we worked so hard to get it!"

"What'll they fill in with if we drop out?" Samson asked.

"There must be fifty-five acts right now on the network standby list just waiting for the other fifty-four entertainers to drop dead!" said Lisle.

"Why can't Dolly and the three of us do the number?" Josh asked. "We've done it before."

The manager shook his head. "Dolly's hands are all cut up. She can't play. But she's going to do the solo ballad instead of Pearl."

That brought a spate of objections, mostly from Josh.

"What if Pearl shows up?" he challenged. "She makes a better appearance."

"Josh," said Lisle, patronizingly, "Dolly has more appeal in her left earlobe than Pearl does in her whole overinflated body."

"Yeah? You're such a good judge of femininity! Well, you're forgetting one little thing, Charlie—the sponsor wants Pearl to do the solo."

"Not anymore, dear boy," Lisle smiled smugly. "Today, Dolly has headline appeal and Pearl is—"

He didn't get to finish the sentence. A scream cut him off. We whirled in the direction of the sound. It was followed by a piercing wail. "Dolly!" I shouted and started off down the corridor. Somehow Josh got ahead of me; rounding the corner, I saw Dolly staring into the open door of Amanda's dressing room. Josh shoved Dolly aside roughly and strode inside. She clutched the jamb with one bandaged hand, slumping against the door frame.

When she saw me, Dolly fell into my arms, sobbing convulsively. I felt her go limp. She had fainted.

In the dressing room, Josh stood over the body of Pearl Boulder. I could tell it was Pearl by the clothes she'd worn the night before and by the color of her hair. I would never have recognized her face. Most of it had been shot away.

18

"It's a goddamned epidemic!" Cass growled, slamming the door. He strode over to the cot in the corner and sat heavily upon it. The combined pressure of trying to cope with the Boulder Clan mess and also to handle Nashville's carnival season madness was wearing the deputy down.

He'd spent plenty of time talking to the Clan. Now that he had finished, Cass asked Hilary and me to step inside the fatal dressing room. She sat in a chair near the makeup mirror while I remained standing, leaning against the wall near the door.

"This time," the deputy told us, "we've got tabs on the whole rotten bunch . . . and a hell of a lot of good it does!"

"Would you mind running it down for me?" Hilary asked. "We were in the middle of it, so I suppose you have us clocked, too."

Cass nodded. "Uh–huh. You know about Dolly since you dropped her off last night at the station house and later picked her up."

"The thing I wonder about," I said, "is whether Dolly's near-poisoning directly set up Pearl's shooting."

"How do you mean?" the deputy asked.

"Maybe because Dolly took the flask, the killer had to resort to a pistol. The liquor may have been meant for Pearl in the first place."

Hilary was staring impatiently at me; I asked her what was wrong, and she told me I was. I thought of a few things I'd like to tell her, but decided to keep it civilized for Cass's sake.

"Okay," he continued, "the M.E. figures the murder took place sometime between 10:00 P.M. and midnight. Now here's the rundown on everyone's whereabouts during that time."

He handed Hilary a notebook with a timetable scribbled in it. I looked over her shoulder and read it, ignoring the entries pertaining to myself and Hilary.

BRIAN LUCAS: Arrived Tootsie's 9:12 P.M. with Samson
   Boulder. Left Tootsie's 12:45 A.M. Returned Ramada Inn.

There was a note in Cass's handwriting:

   Tootsie's back door faces Opry. Not under constant surveillance.

I asked the deputy about it.

"We had three men assigned, one for each vehicle, and a fourth for Lisle—that was all I could spare. When all of you converged on Tootsie's, they were able to stake out both exits, but not before."

So Brian wasn't eliminated. I continued to read the timetable.

DOLLY BOULDER: Arrived 9:55 P.M. precinct H.Q. Picked up same 11:33 P.M. Returned to Ramada Inn 11:58 P.M.

JOSH BOULDER: Left Lisle's home for Stern's Bar and Grill in company of deceased. Left Stern's 10 P.M. for Grand Ole Opry. Arrived 10:08 P.M. Deceased entered back door of Opry. Walked to Tootsie's Orchid Lounge. Arrived 10:12 P.M. Left 10:39 P.M., walked to Grand Ole Opry. Entered 10:43 P.M. Left 11:03 P.M. Drove to Ramada Inn; went to room for rest of night.

CHARLES LISLE: Unobserved leaving home all night.

SAMSON BOULDER: Arrived Tootsie's 9:12 P.M. with Brian Lucas. Thrown out of Tootsie's 11:26 P.M. Walked to Pussycat Club 11:29 P.M. arrival.

There was another note in the margin:

Pussycat—three exits. Insufficient surveillance.
Thrown out of Pussycat 11:58 P.M.

There were several other similar entries. Samson ended up in the VW sleeping it off by 2:15.

"So," said Hilary, studying the timetable, "the field really hasn't been narrowed down."

Cass shook his head. "Josh is the most likely choice at this point. He was actually observed entering the Opry, where he stayed for some time. Yet Samson and Lucas can't be eliminated either."

"Hold it a minute before we go on from Josh," Hilary said. "Did he give any reason for going to the Opry?"

"Uh–huh. The first time he claims Pearl got an anonymous phone call asking her to drop by. The second time, he was impatient to find Pearl, but he claims that she was nowhere in sight. . . ."

"Which is probably a fabrication," said Hilary. "Either he killed her, or he found the body and was too scared to report it."

Cass agreed to the possibilities, but remarked that Charlie Lisle bugged him more than anyone else in the case at that point.

"Why him?" I asked.

"Because he *seems* to be a hundred percent in the clear—yet he went ahead and gave the solo to Dolly this morning, even though Pearl hadn't yet been found. Sound suspicious?"

"Possibly," Hilary mused. "Of course, a killer who can murder people with indetectable poison and slip notes under doors without being seen might not have much trouble firing a pistol by proxy."

Cass gave her a sour look.

"How reliable," I asked, "is the man you assigned to cover Lisle?"

"He's A–OK," Cass stated, "but Lisle's home is big. It's not inconceivable that he could have slipped out without being seen—it's pretty dark in that neck of the woods; only he couldn't have taken his car. . . ."

We talked a while longer, but nothing new was revealed.

Hilary and I discussed the case later over lunch at the Spanola where I had an excellent omelette made with baby cactus. Hilary sipped a Margarita and avoided food on the theory that her brain functions better when her body is cheated of sustenance.

"The thing that worries me," I said, "is that the attempt on Dolly may not have been an accident—in which case, the killer will try again."

"That's definitely a possibility," Hilary nodded. "The trouble is none of the motives seem to tally. Anyone who wanted Amanda dead wouldn't go after Pearl *and* Dolly, too, would they?"

"Why not?" I asked, spearing a green tube of cactus flesh. "If one of the *men* wanted the solo spot—"

"Oh, come on, Gene, do you *really* think anyone would embark on a mass-murder spree just for three minutes of air time?"

"It's possible."

"Sure, it's possible," she said, licking the salt that rimmed the glass, "but it's not probable—yet any other motives I can think of won't wash."

"Such as?"

"Say, for instance, that Samson hated Pearl enough to kill her. All right, but he seemed to get along well with Dolly and Amanda."

"One may smile and smile and be a villain."

"Mmm—hmm, but I don't think Samson's that subtle. Lisle, on the other hand, supposedly hates women, but he wouldn't let that interfere with his professional decisions."

"Last night," I remarked, "I tried to chart out the means and opportunity for everybody involved. I didn't get very far."

"Well," said Hilary, "at least they've got the bullets that killed Pearl. I wonder who has a license for a gun? Shooting was a mistake—it could trip up the killer by pure, run-of-the-mill police work."

"I don't know, Hilary. What with the magic tricks he's already pulled, I wouldn't be surprised if the killer's shells don't have any marks on them."

Hilary became motionless, staring intently into space.

"Gene," she said abruptly, "get the check. I have to get back to the motel."

"What's up?"

"I *think* you just gave me an idea. . . ." Blotting her lips, she rose.

"Hilary," I said, irked, "would you *please* do me a favor? Don't start the great-detective-keeps-his-own-counsel act! Let me in on what you're thinking."

"No," Hilary said. "Not yet—I'm sorry." She turned and started out. I addressed a few choice epithets to her retreating back.

At the motel, Hilary asked me to stick around since she would probably have to run over to the Opry again later. I said I'd be in my room.

When I got there, I saw a flashing red light on the phone. It meant there was a message for me at the main desk.

I hoped it was from Harry MacArthur.

19

It was.

The reporter had single-spaced the story over a couple of sheets of paper. The heading read:

"PECULIAR POISON PRODUCES DEADLY ACCURATE TIMETABLE"

No byline was given, but Harry had penciled in the date and page number of the story; otherwise he added no comment:

Nobody knows how many deaths have resulted from the use of the weird poison, camotillo, often known as "the calendar of death."

The root of this parasitic Latin American vine has been used for centuries by natives of Central and South America to get rid of political enemies or to murder rivals for the love of a jungle princess.

The properties of camotillo have baffled every toxicologist who has studied it.

Only the potato-shaped root is poisonous. It is dug up,

tagged with the digging date, and dried. The digging date is of vital importance to the would-be assassin.

The root is ground and mixed with food or drink. It is lethal in all cases—unless the victim drinks tea made from the vine's leaves prior to the death date.

Nothing else can counteract the deadly poison, and this in itself is a medical oddity.

But the thing that makes camotillo one of the most bizarre instruments of death is its time-clock or calendar element. By this, an assassin can poison his victim today—yet cause him to die on a definite date in the future.

The time element hinges on the date between the digging of the root and the administration of the poison. For example, if the murderer wants the man to die in exactly one month, he administers the poison from a root dug up thirty days previously.

The same thing applies whether the period chosen is two weeks or six months.

In the forefront of those scientists trying to pinpoint the secrets of camotillo is Robert LeMaire, who has spent 20 years combing remote regions of the world in search of plants that kill—and cure!

While collecting data for pharmaceutical research, LeMaire has become a keen observer of many remarkable medical feats performed by *brujos*, or witch doctors, using plants and herbs unknown to the outside world.

"I've witnessed unbelievable cures by these old *brujos*. The trackless rain forests of Central and South America hold many untapped secrets that one day may bring revolutionary changes in the science of medicine," explained LeMaire.

"The records of camotillo I've been able to examine," he said, "show that death came to each victim within one or two days of the stipulated date.

"In all cases where the poison was suspected and the antidote given, the victims lived with no ill effects," LeMaire added.

"The big question mark," he said, "is how a deadly poison can lie dormant in a human body for months on end, give no indication whatsoever of its presence, and then kill on a pre-determined day!"

The answer to that question eludes modern science.

I read it a second time, astounded. If this mystery substance poisoned Amanda Boulder, it could have been administered to her long before I joined the Clan on the road. It would be a very neat answer for the problem of the undetectable toxin.

But who could possibly know about such an obscure drug? Samson remarked once that *GRIT* was his favorite newspaper, so it made sense that the Clan might have read the article in question. But simply knowing about camotillo wouldn't be enough: Access to it would mean a trip to Central or South America.

I called Hilary and read the piece to her. She was equally astonished and asked me to read it a second time before commenting. "That," she said at last, "is the weirdest thing I've ever heard. It sounds like it was written during the silly season."

"What do you think?" I asked. "Should I tell Joe Cass about it?"

"Not yet. He's got enough headaches. Why don't you try to establish its authenticity?"

"Okay, will do. When do you want me to take you over to the Opry?"

"In about a half-hour. Is that enough time?"

I said it was, then hung up and got right back on the phone. It took me a while to track down Harry MacArthur, but I finally got hold of him. Thanking him for transcribing the story, I asked whether he could find out who'd written it for *GRIT*, and if any source material on file told how to get in touch with the scientist mentioned in the article, Robert LeMaire.

"It ran some time ago, Gene," Harry said, "so I don't know if I'll have any luck, but I'll see what I can do. Call you back."

The next thing I did was to phone long distance to the chief toxicologist of the New York Medical Examiner's office. Finding someone who could answer my questions was a good trick, but I finally got hold of a friendly assistant and explained my problem. He couldn't offer any help. He had never heard of camotillo. However, he suggested I call the tropical plants specialist at the Manhattan Botanical Gardens. "And if you do," the toxicologist added, "*and* if he's heard of this stuff, would you let *me* know about it?"

I said I would, rang off, and tried to call the botanical expert. He wasn't in, and it took some persuading to convince his secretary to provide the number where he could be reached. After twenty minutes of red tape, wrong numbers and busy signals, I finally had him on the line—only to find that he'd never heard of camotillo, either.

"It sounds organically related to one of the arrow-poison roots," he remarked, "but the time-clock property is incredible. I'm sure I would have remembered it if I'd ever read anything about it. Sorry."

I had one last possibility. Looking up a Philadelphia number in my book, I called Marty Gold, an old friend of mine who was resident pharmacist at the Pennsylvania General Clinic at Tenth and Oxford and had once studied at Philadelphia College of Pharmacy and Science. Since it was

Saturday, I had to phone him at home. His wife answered.

"Gene!" she said, delighted. "Where are you? In town?"

"Uh–uh. Nashville. I've got a problem. Is Marty there?"

"Are you kidding?" she laughed. "Where else would he be on Saturday afternoon?"

I knew what she meant. Gold's chief passion in life, other than his wife, is collecting old phonograph records. He had an enormous assortment of Dixieland, personality, and jazz 78s, and every Saturday he ensconced himself in his basement for several hours so he could revel in the past. It took his wife, Louise, five minutes to get him to the phone: He'd been listening to a speech of President McKinley's and felt it would have been rude to walk out on such an important personage. I read the article to him and told him what I wanted to know.

"That's quite a drug," he said. "I could make a fortune dispensing it!"

"Have you ever heard of it?"

"No, but it's not exactly the sort of thing you read about in the Smith, Kline and French catalog. Give me a couple of hours. I'll track it down in one of the pharmacopoeias. What did you say the name of the toxicologist was?"

"Robert LeMaire."

"Okay," he said, "if he's as big in the field as the story implies, he ought to have a paper or two kicking around in one of the libraries. I'll try the Free Library on the Parkway, and I'll run on over to PCP and S. Give me a number where I can reach you." Marty asked me to keep an eye out for any old record sales while I was in Nashville, then rang off. I dialed Hilary's room, told her what I'd done and asked whether she was ready to go.

"Yes. When you come over, bring the press clippings on the Boulder Clan."

"Right. I'll be there in a minute."

I stuffed the clips into the folder and took them over to Hilary's room. She asked me to drop them on her bed so she could read them later.

"How are you coming?" I asked. "Have you got the mess untangled by now?"

"Not completely," she replied. "I have to ask a few more questions."

"I'm worried that Dolly may still be in danger."

She shook her head. "I doubt it. I don't think the killer's planning any more violence."

"Then you know who it is."

"I can make a good guess," Hilary said, cryptically refusing to do so. It's a wonder Watson didn't murder Sherlock Holmes.

I drove Dolly's car to the Opry and waited while Hilary spoke with Lisle. That annoyed me because Hilary motioned me off in a peremptory fashion. When the meeting broke up, I collared the manager so I could clarify a point I'd been wondering about.

"When Pappy Boulder was killed in the car accident," I asked, "who was behind the wheel?"

"Amanda," he replied.

I thanked him, then caught up with Hilary, who was talking in the dressing room corridor with Josh.

"That's what *I* heard," she said to him. "If you want to refute it, now's the time."

"Look," he told her, "I've had it with your prying. People can talk all they want, that's their business, but I'm saying nothing, understand?"

"You're a damned fool," Hilary told him. He started to

walk away, but her next question made him freeze in his tracks.

"Has anything been stolen from you?"

He didn't turn around until he could compose his face the way he wanted it. When he did look at Hilary, Josh scuffed a shoe against the floor and grinned, "Shucks, ma'am, I'm just a country boy. I don't know what you mean. . . ."

Hilary sniffed and disdainfully walked away.

As soon as her back was turned, Josh's smile disappeared. He glared at Hilary with pure malice. Then, remembering that I was still watching, Josh looked me in the eye and forced himself to grin with an assumed jocularity.

"Man," he said, "I bet anybody who crawls in the sack with *her* has to prime her first with antifreeze!"

I didn't respond. After an awkward pause, he turned abruptly and walked out of the corridor.

I asked Hilary whether she needed to talk to anyone else.

"No," she answered, "I'm about satisfied. There's still one detail I have to mull over, and then I'll have this business solved."

"What detail is that?"

"What did the killer put in the water that Amanda drank?"

"Oh, is *that* all?" I asked ironically. "Lots of luck, Hilary, lots of luck!"

20

In a recent Sunday edition of *The New York Times*, Ryman Auditorium was described architecturally as "a vernacular version of the Ruskinian Gothic—a style with a high casualty rate . . ." and, sure enough, forces were already well under way to transfer the home of the Grand Ole Opry out of the Ryman and across the river into Opryland U.S.A.—a sort of country-western amusement park that Walt Disney might have cherished. The Ryman's owner, National Life and Accident Insurance Company, had earmarked the building for demolition, thus stirring up a storm of protest from people and organizations who demanded that the Ryman be preserved as a historic landmark.

The fact that it would be one of the last such occasions at the Ryman, together with the usual carnival brouhaha of the awards telecast, contrived to jam the nonairconditioned auditorium to overflowing. Hilary and I could not get seats closer to the stage than in the press section at the front of the "Confederate balcony," a gallery so named because it was built in 1897 to accommodate a reunion of southern Civil War veterans; it later had been strengthened with many more steel beams than were required by safety regulations, and an intricate network of dovetailed wooden timbers supported it.

The afternoon editions of the local papers had been rushed into an extra printing to cover Pearl's murder, Dolly's poisoning and her subsequent recovery, and her intended appearance on the evening telecast. TV news shows had been bruiting the Boulder case, too; as a result, the atmosphere in the press section that night was knife-keen.

"How can she get herself together after what happened?" one columnist asked. "*I* couldn't make a sound!"

"I hear," said an agency executive, "they had to scrap the Boulders' group number."

I wished I could have been backstage to help bolster Dolly's confidence, and, more to the point, to stand guard. But the dressing rooms were in turmoil as early as 7:30, and I would have really been in the way, so I sat upstairs with Hilary and tried not to feel too apprehensive.

At precisely 9:00 P.M. Central Standard Time, the band struck up a brassy overture based on the "Wabash Cannonball." I heard a flurry of rustling sounds and saw several journalists extract score sheets and smooth them out on their briefcases. Each sheet had a rundown of the various awards to be presented that evening. Ample blank space opposite each category permitted the writer to pencil in the name of the winner when it was revealed during the broadcast.

"Tennessee" Ernie Ford was host, and he began the proceedings with a chorus of "Sixteen Tons," followed by "Mule Skinner Blues," after which he traded quips with the first award presenter, Chet Atkins. He, in turn, announced the year's top instrumentalist, and after the victor had paraded before the camera, the Bair Family trooped onstage to sing a quick medley of their hits. A commercial followed.

The procession continued in similar fashion: cornpone humor between the M.C. and guests, followed by a succession of singers and songwriters trotting up to the podium to claim a polished-wood trophy that looked like a petrified banana. Between awards, brief musical numbers and advertisements altered the pace.

"And now, friends and neighbors, let's give a special welcome to the next little girl. The fact that she's here at all tonight gives a new meaning to the old worn-out notion that the show must go on. . . . Here she is . . . Miss Dolly Boulder!"

Thunderous applause. As Dolly stepped onstage, several people in the balcony stood up, and soon, the whole auditorium (or as much as I could see of it) was on its feet, according her a standing ovation.

I marveled at her stamina. The events of the previous night had left me exhausted, but Dolly was riding on a crest of energy: She smiled with just the right combination of perkiness and melancholy. But I hardly recognized her. Someone with antiquated ideas of glamour had been at her during the afternoon, and the results were outrageous; the gown she wore hid her trim hips and overaccentuated the bustline. Her hair was frosted in a cloying upsweep.

The musical introduction began, and Dolly sang her sister's song. As soon as the crowd recognized the number, it indulged in a brief, but spirited, round of applause. Dolly interpreted the ballad with considerable slickness and economy of expression; though it wasn't the way Amanda would have sung it, it was still far better than I would have imagined. In the short time Dolly'd had to prepare it she'd brought considerable artistry to bear. If she could do so much in one afternoon, it wouldn't take her long to become a first-class stylist.

There was a sudden grip on my knee. Turning to Hilary, I saw a curiously intent expression on her face. As the song ended and the auditorium filled with a deafening noise of applause, foot-stamping, shouts, and an occasional cry of "bravo," Hilary rose.

"What's wrong?" I asked, putting my mouth near her ear in order to be heard above the din. She shook her head and tried to say something, but it was no use—the auditory competition was too keen. Hilary made her way along the row and reached the central aisle. I started to follow her, but she motioned me to stay where I was as she left the balcony. I didn't see her again that evening.

The only word I'd been able to make out when she tried to speak above the noise of the applause was "sick."

The crowds were so thick after the show I couldn't get backstage to see Dolly. I waited at the rear entrance, hoping to catch her on the way out, but after I'd stood there several minutes, jostled by autograph-seekers, Brian saw me and pushed his way over.

"She's already gone," he said.

"Where?"

"Roger Miller's. Big party. Come on, you can ride over with me and Samson."

It took another few minutes to find the giant, but once we did, we had no further trouble getting to the VW—no one stood in Samson's path. We piled into the bus and Samson pulled into traffic—of which there was plenty. It took us quite some time to get to the King of the Road, Miller's plush Nashville motel. The ride was a quiet one. Brian, as usual, had nothing to say, while Samson confined his conversation to Monday morning quarterbacking of the country-music awards, explaining to me who really should have won.

The party was quintessentially southern—a tiny suite of rooms engaged to accommodate a crowd of several hundred: It was like the Lexington Avenue subway at 5:30 in the afternoon.

Though we'd started late, the three of us still arrived earlier than Dolly. It took ten minutes to shove through the bodies and another five to convince the bartender that I existed. Just as I got my hands around a glass, there was a sudden increase in the volume of chatter, then a hush.

"Dolly Boulder."

She entered on Josh's arm. Someone started to applaud. Everyone crowded around the pair, plying them with questions, congratulations, condolences.

I turned to the bartender and ordered a drink for Dolly, then worked my way forward. When she saw me, she flashed a smile at me and reached for the drink. "Gene," she said, "thanks *so* much . . ." then turned to talk to a reporter.

"I don't know yet," she told him. "Josh and I have been talking it over. We *might* go out on the road together. . . ."

I looked at Josh. He had the same broad grin on his face as always, but for a change, he let Dolly do the talking and contributed nothing to the interview. He simply stood there, smiling like an automaton.

They left together half an hour later. I never got a chance to congratulate Dolly.

21

The Boulder tragedy rushed to its bloody conclusion on Sunday, though I never would have guessed the climax was so near by the sluggish way in which the day began. But before it was over, I had to make another trip to Nashville General, this time to have a bullet extracted from my arm.

Yet Sunday morning started quietly. I was tired from Saturday's exertions and slept late. When I woke, I stayed in bed, staring at the ceiling. A whisper of rain traced thin lines down the windowpanes, and I listened to the intimate sound for a long time.

I began to form a theory about the murderer and how Amanda had been killed. I turned it over in my mind, examined it from various viewpoints, deciding that it might be viable.

There was a tap at the door. It was Hilary. Reluctantly, I rose and let her in.

"Are you going to sleep all day?" she asked. "What's the matter, aren't you feeling well?"

I shrugged; closing the door, I walked to an armchair and

sat down. Hilary had the sheaf of press clippings with her. She took it to the bureau, set it down, then turned and regarded me. "What happened? Did you and Dolly have an argument?"

I shook my head. "I didn't even get near her last night. She was busy being famous."

"I'm not surprised," Hilary said, sitting on the edge of the bed. "Dolly's been waiting to be an Opry star for years."

"How do you know?"

"Oh, *come on!* Practically the first thing she said when you met her was how good a singer she is. Didn't you wonder when she asked you to hear her sing right away, even though you'd scarcely even said hello?"

"Wonder about what?"

"About suggesting the two of you meet the very first night after the show. Why do you think she made such a suggestion? Surely you don't have *that* high an opinion of your masculine charm?!"

I was in no mood for Hilary's brand of ego-mangling. "All right," I said, "what do you attribute it to? What did Dolly have to gain being nice to me?"

"You might become her PR man. Even Pearl showed interest. It's smart to get on good terms with somebody who can slant press releases."

"Do me a favor, Hilary. Go away."

"No," she said harshly, "snap out of it! You've hardly known her a week, and you're acting like a stupid adolescent."

"Look," I said, "it's none of your damned business—but Dolly and I have no understanding between us, so I don't even want to talk about it."

She shook her head. "She really means a lot to you, doesn't she?"

Ignoring her, I ducked into the bathroom and splashed water on my face and neck. Later, when I returned to the bedroom, shaved and dressed, Hilary was still there.

As I entered the room, she fiddled in her purse, found a scrap of paper, and gave it to me. "That's the number of Joe Cass's testing lab. Call them later."

"I take it you have an idea what was in the water Amanda drank?"

She nodded.

"When did this occur to you?"

"While we were watching the awards ceremony. I got up and called Cass for the number. He authorized a new test on the contents of Amanda's stomach."

"Didn't everything show up the first time?"

"The lab," Hilary explained, "was looking for toxin. It discounted sugars, proteins, and other foodstuffs normally found in the stomach."

"Do you mean Amanda was killed by something that's normally harmless?"

"No," Hilary said, "they identified the poison. Cass is tracing it."

"What is it?"

But before she could reply, the telephone rang.

It was Dolly. She wanted me to come to her room.

"I owe you an apology for last night, Gene."

"No, you don't." I wished Hilary weren't in the room.

"Oh, yes, I do! Please come—it's important."

I said I would, and hung up.

"Where are you going?" Hilary asked.

"Out for a while."

"To see Dolly." It was a statement, not a question.

"I already asked you to mind your own business."

"This *is* my business."

"How do you figure that?"

"Because . . . I want to keep you efficient. I don't want to see you hurt."

"I see," I said sarcastically. "You regard me as a private pincushion."

"I *do* not," she protested.

"Then what do you call that remark about my masculine charm? The only reason you're worried about Dolly is that she might steal your property. It's hard to find whipping boys who'll put up with you."

That made her livid. Her fingers balled into a fist and connected with my jaw. It hurt.

I saw red. Grabbing her wrist, I spun Hilary around, threw an arm over her shoulders, bent her against my out-thrust leg and delivered several sharp smacks to the base of her spine—a politer way of putting it. She cursed and, pulling away, tried to punch me again, but I grabbed her wrist, pulled her close, and squeezed her in a bear hug.

"Let go, damn you!" she gasped, no longer struggling, "you're hurting me!"

"What the hell do you think you did?" I barked, but loosened my grip. She stepped back and stood within the circle of my arms, panting for breath. In spite of my anger, I couldn't help noticing the proximity of Hilary's body.

"Are you going to let go of me?" she asked. I opened my arms and gently, almost involuntarily, brushed her hips with my hands.

And she used her knee on me.

"Give my regards to Dolly," Hilary snapped, slamming the door behind her.

I got up from the floor several minutes later.

22

Dolly rushed into my arms as soon as I entered the room.

"Gene, I feel *terrible*," she said, "treating you like that last night! You must've thought I was playing Little Dolly Superstar!"

"Not at all," I lied.

"You did, too! But Charlie told me to stay with Josh and let the press see the two of us together. I should've figured it out, but I was too excited and I didn't think. I just went along with everything Charlie said—until all of a sudden, I heard Josh saying we're going on the road together, just like he was planning with Amanda and then Pearl! I'll be *damned* if I will, though!" She was vehement.

"Then how come I heard *you*—"

"I know," she said, sitting on the bed. "I had to agree with his story, because he'd been telling every reporter that's what we were going to do, go out touring together. But I'm going to scotch that story first thing, only I couldn't do it last night! It would've been too awkward after Josh'd just finished telling the press—"

"But didn't it sound bad, anyway?" I interrupted. "He'd

only announced his engagement with Amanda two days earlier."

"Yes, but some of our fans weren't too happy when he and I got divorced in the first place. It wasn't—well, Christian. The news that he was going to marry my sister was more shocking to them than last night's announcement, you can be sure." She looked at me gravely. "Gene, can you understand how I could get so confused about what Josh and Charlie were cooking up? I mean, was it wrong of me to become so excited with all the public attention I was getting? Was it okay to—well, enjoy it *a little?*"

"Dolly," I reassured her, "you deserved every single bit of it."

"Thanks," she said, wrinkling up her nose. "I kinda thought so, too."

She looked so damned cute I had to hug her.

"But now," she said softly, putting her arms around me in return, "I have to really apologize for last night."

"You just did."

"Uh-uh. Not enough," she whispered.

Dolly brushed her lips against my cheek and held me tighter. The fabric of her blouse was cool to my touch, and as I caressed her, I could feel the rougher texture of her skirt where the garment dipped beneath her belt. . . .

Later, Dolly asked if I could do a favor for her, and I said she could name it. But I was absolutely unprepared for what she was about to ask.

"Meet me this afternoon in the balcony of the Opry," Dolly requested, "but don't let anybody know you're there. Do you think you can do that?"

"Hold on a minute! What's the mystery all of a sudden? Don't we already have enough?"

"It's Josh," she replied. "I told him late last night that I wasn't going to go on any concert tour with him, but he wouldn't take no for an answer. He insisted on talking it over again today with Charlie, but I refused."

"And?"

"So—I have to show you something." Dolly walked over to the bureau, took a note off the top, and handed it to me.

"Dolly," it read, "let's talk over the tour. We'll leave Charlie out of it. Meet me at four in the Opry balcony. Josh."

I shook my head. "Why such a weird place?"

Dolly shrugged. "Who knows? Probably because the telecast is over and the place will be deserted."

"You think he's afraid to talk about it in public?"

"I *know* him," she said. "He doesn't want the press to learn I even gave the joint tour a second thought. He's supposed to be so damned irresistible—Josh doesn't want his ladykiller image tarnished, especially by a woman who already walked out on him!"

I saw what she meant, and also noticed she found it upsetting to talk about, so I held Dolly close and didn't speak for a long while. Finally, I asked her what she expected me to accomplish by being there in the balcony. Josh would certainly clam up if he spotted me.

"He doesn't have to know you're there," Dolly explained. "There's a projection booth in the back of the auditorium, in the balcony. You could wait in there, and if—"

"*And if*—what?"

"Well," she murmured, evading my gaze, "I'd just feel better if you were there. . . ." She didn't have to say any more. I knew what she meant. I'd recognized the handwriting on the note.

23

There was a message waiting for me back in my room. I dialed the number in Philadelphia and got my friend Marty Gold on the phone.

"Well," I asked, "did you have any luck with camotillo?"

"Where the hell did you come up with this one?" he yelped.

"No information available?"

"Listen, I checked both the American and British pharmacopoeias, the *Merck Index*, standard texts on toxins, a master's thesis on poisonous plants, and the entire card catalog in the college library, not only for camotillo, but for this 'authority,' Robert LeMaire. Not a word on either of them!"

"Okay," I said, "so relax. It's a fake."

"Maybe. But everybody agrees the description sounds plausible."

"*What?*"

"I don't mean the part about the stuff killing according to a timetable. That's fantastic. But the general characterization as a poisonous root sounds likely. There are several toxic tubers in the tropics. *Curare* itself—"

"Never mind," I interrupted, "it won't mean a thing unless I can bring it out of the realm of science fiction. Thanks for the favor, Marty."

"No sweat. But I'm damned if I'm satisfied!"

I suggested he go down to the cellar and play a King Oliver on Gennett to calm down.

After I rang off, I phoned MacArthur to see how his end of the search was going. It wasn't.

"I checked the entire *GRIT* file for the year," he said, "but I'll be damned if I can find who sent the original copy for that piece. But our stringers are reliable. I don't think any of them would make up a story like that. The best thing would be to get in touch with somebody who's an expert in tropical *flora*."

"Thanks, Harry. I can think of just the man, too, but there's no time." I hung up.

So the camotillo hunt was at a standstill. Of course, Hilary claimed the toxin had been identified, but unless it fit the theory I'd formulated earlier that morning, mere knowledge of its name would bring us no closer to knowing how Amanda swallowed it from an untainted glass and pitcher.

Meanwhile, I had a more pressing matter to contend with: Dolly's imminent appointment with Josh Mackenzie.

I didn't know what to do. Should I let the meeting take place, or would it be better and safer for Dolly to steer clear?

Reluctantly, I picked up the phone and called Hilary. I hated to do so after our last scene together, but she was the only one—so she claimed—who was in all but total possession of the facts.

When she heard my voice, she asked how I was feeling

and sounded genuinely contrite. Our recent set-to still rankled, but I refrained from baiting the Dragon Lady and told her matter-of-factly about the four o'clock appointment.

"Should Dolly go through with it?" I asked.

"Yes. There's no danger. When Joe Cass gets the new lab results and traces down a few other details, he'll be able to make an arrest."

I didn't like the self-assured lack of interest in her voice.

"Are you positive it's all right to. . . ."

"I *said* so, didn't I?"

"Okay, Hilary, I'll go along with you. But nothing had better go wrong."

"It won't," she repeated, then hung up.

I hoped she was right, but I was afraid for Dolly's life. Not without reason.

24

If I were in love with amateur heroics, I suppose I would have taken my post in the balcony at 4:00 P.M. and brazened it out myself. But I was more concerned about Dolly's well-being, so I stopped over at the station earlier that afternoon and explained the situation to Joe Cass.

He was as unimpressed as Hilary. "*You* be there," he told me, "and let me know exactly what happens, okay?"

"Aren't you going to stake it out?"

He snorted derisively. "I'm through chasing the Boulders all over Nashville. Next week is the country disc jockey convention, and that's twice as bad as the awards ceremony! Traffic is beyond belief! I'm not pulling any other men off patrol."

"But—"

"But nothing! All I need are a few points of confirmation from the labs, and I move in. The killer's not going to pull anything else. I've got the Clan under general surveillance, and that's plenty good enough."

"Uh–huh," I countered sarcastically, "just like it was in preventing Pearl's death."

The deputy ignored the remark and stolidly refused to set up an extra patrol around the Opry that afternoon. I left the police station, cursing both Cass and Hilary, whose counsel I figured the cop was following.

My visit with Cass had produced one positive result, though. I finally learned what poison had been found in Amanda's stomach.

"It was a real bitch to trace," Cass explained. "The trouble is the stuff's a very common drug, but poisoning from it is extremely rare, so the lab—"

"Never mind the nitty-gritty," I interrupted. "Just tell me its name."

"Pilocarpine hydrochloride. Organic base, from a tropical root."

"What's it used for?"

"Eye drops. Oculists prescribe it for open-angle glaucoma. Relieves pressure on the eye. According to the medical examiner, druggists aren't all that careful, you can get a refill pretty easily."

"Does it leave a trace in water?"

Cass nodded. "You bet it does. Only it wasn't necessarily in the water. I had the lab check for presence of alcohol. There was plenty in her stomach."

"That's impossible," I objected, "Amanda didn't drink anything all morning."

The deputy shrugged. "The booze was there all the same."

I arrived at the Grand Ole Opry at twenty minutes to four. It was raining—a slow, chilly drizzle. I made a fast reconnaissance. The auditorium was practically deserted. The debris created by the crowds that jammed the Ryman on the previous evening had not yet been picked up, but the

TV cables, cameras, and related paraphernalia were cleared away, and an energetic stage crew had already dismantled the thrust apron, so that the proscenium standing Sunday afternoon was smaller and farther away from the front row of seats than the one I'd seen earlier.

The night before, the Opry had been stifling hot, in spite of the autumn weather, but as I climbed to the balcony that afternoon, I shivered. The wind cut through the interstices in the wood paneling; the slight but steady rain added icy moisture to the atmosphere. The place felt like a rustic boathouse.

The Confederate balcony was built on a steep rake and the first row of seats now overhung the open space on the auditorium floor in front of the proscenium lip. I couldn't look down without experiencing vertigo. At the back of the balcony, an aisle ran the width of the house and at points was interrupted by doorways opening onto stairways leading to the main floor. In the very center of the rear wall, between two of these doors, there was a structural protrusion with a pair of narrow windows set high in its exterior face. It had to be the projection booth that Dolly told me to use as a hiding place.

I skirted the balcony and found a door beneath the protruding segment. Opening it, I spied a steep staircase twisting up in the direction of the windows. I entered and closed the door behind me. I was alone in darkness. Passing my hand along the wall, I tried to find a light switch, but having no luck, decided to grope my way up. Putting my hand out, I grasped a dusty bannister and slowly mounted the stairs. At first, I couldn't see a thing, but soon the wan light filtering through the booth's windows afforded me minimal illumination—enough to enable me to keep my feet on the steps without breaking my neck. At last, I reached the top.

Still holding onto the rail, I tried to discern some detail in the dim surroundings. The outlines of a pair of 35mm cameras, one behind each window, were visible in the feeble light, but everything else was cloaked in shadow.

I wasn't alone. Outside, the Opry was quiet, but in this chamber, which should have been totally hushed, I heard the gentlest of sounds and knew someone was in the room with me. I demanded to know who was there.

"Who did you expect?" a familiar voice asked. Emerging from the gloom, Hilary Quayle stepped into the moted light that crept in through the twin openings. I blinked, startled at her appearance. She was wearing blue satin trousers and a low-cut silken blouse that clung to her petite frame. Her blonde hair had been loosed from its customary back-knot and hung down to her shoulders, framing her face. She looked at me uncertainly, waiting for me to speak. I said nothing.

"Well?" she demanded at last.

I swallowed, not trusting myself to speak.

"Do you like it?" she asked, smiling uncertainly.

"What's the occasion?" I countered, trying to remain cool.

"I just wanted to apologize. . . ."

"All right," I said, "apology accepted." Then I moved quickly past her to one of the apertures, glancing at my watch. It was ten minutes to four.

Coming behind me, Hilary rested her hand on my shoulder and said, "We'll watch together."

"I thought you told me nothing was going to happen."

"Nothing will."

I turned to face her. "Then why are you here?"

"Why? Am I in the way?" I noticed for the first time that she was wearing a subtle, tantalizing scent.

"Look," I demanded, "you're up to something. What is it?"

"I came here to help. Is that *so* hard to believe? Do you want me to leave?"

I shook my head. Frankly, I didn't know how to cope with the situation. I'd been working for Hilary a number of months, and I knew she didn't use perfume. The calculated allure of her outfit, too, was alien to her style, and, though I'd often suggested it, she never wore her hair down. No, the look she was affecting had to be some kind of attempt to copy someone else's notion of feminine beauty—which was absurd, since Hilary was quite attractive, even when she was being her most abrasive self. But then, I'd always suspected that Hilary was completely unable to assess her status with the opposite sex.

I decided to accept her at her word, and act as if she merely wanted to help me watch for Dolly and Josh. Returning to the window, I scanned the balcony, but saw no sign of either one. As I stared through the narrow aperture, she slipped around in front of me and looked through the same window. She might have had a clearer point of vantage from the adjacent projector-slit, and I was about to point that out when she asked me what time it was.

"Five minutes of four. They'll be here any minute."

Hilary nodded, leaning forward to get a better view through the opening. As she did, I felt the gentle brush of her hips against mine. She didn't move away and the two of us stood there, faintly touching in an intimacy so subtle that I was sure she was unaware of it. Yet I couldn't help but sense her body's warmth.

"Gene," she said, her voice barely audible, "are you still angry about what happened before?"

"No, I'm not mad." I had difficulty keeping my voice even. "I guess I was at fault."

"No, you weren't," she said, nestling nearer. There could no longer be any doubt of our physical proximity. "You don't really know why I was so angry. How could you? You're still—" She paused. I thought she would say more, but for some reason, Hilary remained silent. A long time passed; neither of us commented on the secret balance we shared, nor did she attempt to alter it. In the quiet room, the stillness was disturbed by no sound but our breathing.

Then, without sacrificing any tactile intimacy, Hilary turned and rested her hands lightly on my arms. Her lips were slightly parted. . . . And then I heard the footsteps on the balcony.

"Don't pay any attention," Hilary said, not moving.

But I was already looking over her shoulder. Through the slit in the wall, I saw Dolly walking down one of the aisles; when she reached the lowest row, she turned and rested against the parapet. Her mouth was set in a nervous smile. I stuck my hand in the window and moved it from side to side, hoping she could see the movement.

Apparently, she did. Dolly's smile widened just a bit and she touched her fingertips fleetingly to her lips. There was a quick intake of breath from Hilary.

"She's so damned obvious," she snapped.

"You shouldn't talk about being obvious, Hilary," I said coldly, marveling at the rapidity with which our private moment had faded.

"Dolly is ten years older than you," she said, "and even though she pretends to be drippy-sweet—"

"For Christ's sake, Hilary," I interrupted, "let's get our relationship straight, once and for all! What kind of property do you think I am? A secretary or—"

"*Shut up!*" she ordered. Then she glanced down at the clothes she was wearing and gestured contemptuously. "Look at me! Just like that whore—"

"Who does *that* mean?" I demanded.

"You know damned well *who!*" Hilary stamped across the room, reached the top of the stairs, then gave me a withering stare. "I'm *very* sorry I came up here. It was a mistake. We're going to forget everything we said and did—*understand?*"

I nodded. "In other words, your definition of me is 'chattel.' Now butt out of my personal life!"

"Gladly," she snapped, starting down the stairs. But before she'd taken two steps, we heard angry voices outside and the sound of a struggle. Dolly screamed. I ran to the window and saw a figure who must have been Josh wrestling with her on the edge of the balcony. She clutched at him, trying to keep her balance. They swayed. . . .

"Get out of the way!" I yelled, shoving Hilary aside. Scrambling down the stairs in the darkness, I lost my footing, grabbed at the railing but missed, and slipping, landed with a clatter at the bottom of the steps. My left foot twisted under me, and a stab of pain shot through the ankle. But I got up, wincing, opened the balcony door and stumbled through, ignoring the injury.

Dolly was no longer visible. I heard racing footsteps: The man was at the top of the aisle heading for the downstairs opening. I couldn't see his face.

Behind me, Hilary ran down the aisle to the lowermost row and looked over the edge. Her hand jerked to her mouth. She turned to me, a look of sick horror in her eyes. I started down the aisle.

"Gene," she cried, "stay there. Don't look!"

"You claimed nothing would happen to Dolly!" I shouted.

She stood there, miserable, unable to speak.

I heard the assailant on the main floor of the Opry, running toward the stage.

"Get an ambulance!" I roared at Hilary, heading for the stairs, which I took three at a time. My ankle throbbed, but I ignored it. As I reached ground-floor level, I saw a closing door at the side of the stage—the entrance to the dressing rooms. I hurried toward it.

I tried not to look at Dolly's twisted body as I ran, but I couldn't help but see her out of the corner of my eye. There was blood on her face.

Wrenching the door to the corridor open, I practically ran into Samson Boulder.

"What the hell's going on?" he demanded.

"Quick!" I gasped, "help Dolly!" I pointed toward the auditorium door, then began to run again. Over my shoulder, I asked whether Samson had seen Josh.

"He nearly ran me down!" he called. "Keep going. He was running out to the parking lot. . . ."

As I reached the back door, I got my first good look at Josh. He was getting into his car. I could tell by the way he was panting that he'd been running. I yelled for him to stop. When he saw me, he slammed his door and gunned the motor. His face was white.

I hobbled over to Dolly's Thunderbird, scrambled in, stuck the key in the ignition and started the car. Josh was already racing out of the lot and heading down Fifth Avenue toward Broadway. I pushed hard on the gas pedal and shot out after him into traffic.

25

By then, of course, I'd tagged Josh as the killer. There were still loose ends, but I figured Hilary and Cass could resolve them.

I'd recognized Josh's handwriting on both notes: the one that lured Dolly to the cemetery and the other that summoned her to the Opry balcony. The thing that disturbed me was that Dolly still cared enough for her ex-husband to destroy the first note and to smash the flask she must have snitched from him, making it impossible to check for his fingerprints.

One thing I was sure of, even though I didn't know it as a fact: If the bottle were his, so was the missing gun that killed Pearl. I remembered the malevolent glare he'd given Hilary when she asked him whether any of his property was missing.

Josh was right on the scene when Pearl was murdered, whereas the rest of the Clan all had some kind of alibi. Dolly's poisoning might have been an accident, but the only thing that probably saved her from physical attack in the cemetery was the fact that I'd come along with her. By the time he went for her in the balcony, he'd evidently grown desperate; in such an unconcealed position, he must have known he was risking observation. But by then, Dolly must have become such a threat to him that he had no choice: She knew who wrote the notes, who owned the flask. Surely she must also be aware that Josh possessed a gun.

But the thing I couldn't figure out was why Josh would kill both Pearl *and* Amanda. He'd slept with Pearl for some time, but that didn't stop him from desiring Amanda, even though she was the least attractive of the three sisters . . . or maybe it was *because* he was a stud that he had to score with all three of the Boulder sisters. But that gave him no motive for murdering Pearl and Amanda.

He certainly wouldn't have killed them to move up to the lead position in the act. That was absurd. His political tactics were clear: Wooing Amanda, he told her lies about her late husband, planning to attach himself to her career like a barnacle when she—

Mental set!

It came clear in an instant. There was a good reason why I had been unable to reconcile Josh's killing both sisters. He didn't poison Amanda: Pearl did. Nothing else made sense. The younger sister, furious at losing Josh—both personally and professionally—must have decided to get rid of the competition. Then Josh shot her. Simple revenge?

That was an answer only Josh could supply. But I had to catch him first.

He led me a merry chase all over Nashville. Despite the rain that poured down from the slate-colored sky, Josh ignored the hazardous condition of the road, not to mention the speed laws, pedestrians, and traffic lights. Cutting in and out of the moving stream of cars, he aimed the Lincoln over double lines and around acute curves at suicidal speeds. But he couldn't evade my pursuit.

A keening wail arose behind me, and I recognized the nasal whine of a police siren. I paid no attention. Josh abruptly made a wide turn into a side street and shot off at a right angle from the direction in which we'd been traveling. I cursed and swung the wheel, thanking my luck that there were no vehicles approaching in the opposite lane of the street; I had to spin far into it. The wheels skidded. I lurched to one side, righted the irrational curve, then jammed the pedal to the floor and zoomed after Josh. . . .

How had the poison been administered to Amanda?

That was the crucial question, I told myself. But I could imagine two possibilities.

Number one: camotillo, chemically confused in the lab for pilocarpine. Both were organic poisons derived from Latin American plants. Camotillo could have been put in anything that Amanda ate or drank weeks before she sang at the Opry. Josh and Dolly once went to South America on vacation: Might they have brought some back?

The second option, of course, was pilocarpine itself, if it had a toxic effect when administered subcutaneously. Pearl could have smeared some on a deliberately created sliver on the edge of the drinking glass, one that would have cut her sister's mouth upon using the tumbler. When Amanda doubled over that day, her lip was bleeding. The telltale portion of the rim probably was shattered beyond recognition when the glass fell to the stage.

But where did the pilocarpine come from in the first place? Josh wore glasses, of course; did he have glaucoma?

And what about the liquor in Amanda's stomach: Did it come from the same bottle that Dolly drank from?

Loose ends.

The patrol car—judging from the noise of its siren—moved up behind me pretty quickly, but I couldn't see it in the rear-view mirror. The rain was slashing down too hard. Meanwhile, I'd narrowed the gap between the Thunderbird and the Lincoln. I noticed Josh was slowing down, and I also began to recognize the highway he'd taken. . . .

Suddenly, the Ramada loomed up in the distance. Josh raced the Lincoln into the parking lot entrance and braked in front of a lateral row of motel rooms. He jumped out, running across the pavement toward a flight of stairs.

I pulled in next to the Lincoln, swung my legs out of the car, immediately grabbing onto the outer door handle, staggering. I'd forgotten about my ankle. The rain was now a torrent. A wall of water soaked my clothes, drenching me to the skin. I waited for the ache in my ankle to subside, then pushed away from the car and limped to the stairs, seizing the right-hand bannister. The siren grew louder. Trying to keep my weight off my injured foot, I hauled myself up the stairs.

They led to the second level of motel rooms. An open corridor ran the length of the building; it had a concrete floor and a ceiling that overhung the walkway, which did not prevent the rain from dashing sheets of water down the hall. An iron balcony acted as a parapet; I grabbed it tightly so I wouldn't slip, and began to stumble along the corridor.

Josh, about thirty feet away, was emerging from his room, stuffing a wad of bills into a pocket. Without much cash, he must have realized he wouldn't get far in his flight. It was the only sensible explanation for the strange fact that, in spite of pursuit, he'd returned to the motel, risking capture. *Or was it?* Wasn't there something incriminating that he had to get rid of? . . .

I'd forgotten about the gun.

"Stay away, boy!" he shouted over the noise of the rain. For once, he wasn't grinning. "I'll use this if I have to!"

"Just like you used it on Pearl?"

"I have to get rid of it!" he yelled, backing away.

I held my ground.

Josh had almost reached the stairwell. When he turned to start down, I leaped forward in pursuit. More amateur heroics. All I could see was Dolly's broken body, her bloody face. . . .

He caught the movement, spun around, and fired. The bullet slammed into my arm and knocked me back against the railing. He aimed for another shot, but his foot slipped and I heard the shell shatter a window near me. I hoped nobody was in that room.

Josh got to his feet quickly and scrambled down the stairs. I followed, but the combined liabilities of wounded arm and throbbing ankle slowed me down. By the time I reached the ground level, he had sprinted halfway across the parking lot. I could barely see him.

Suddenly, I realized he'd taken the wrong direction and was running away from where he'd parked. There was a swimming pool dividing the motel grounds. He'd run around its edge and was in a dead-end corner of the lot, an area without exit driveways that was surrounded by a high storm fence. Josh was in a cul-de-sac.

I began rounding the pool, but progress was slow. My arm burned, and I was soon gasping for breath. Still, he couldn't go anywhere, so I felt no real need to rush. A strong wind began to drive long slants of rain in my face. I couldn't see Josh, but knew he couldn't be far away. Somewhere behind me, a voice shouted. I ignored it, even though it was calling my name. There was a more urgent sound to pay attention to somewhere up ahead. I realized, with a start, why Josh hadn't tried to get back in the Lincoln.

He was driving the VW bus—straight at me. He must have used up most of the Lincoln's fuel supply in the chase. The noise of the motor grew louder, and I saw the outline of the vehicle in the mist. It was moving slowly and Josh had switched on the dim beams. I realized he wasn't trying to run me down but only wanted to find the gravel driveway so he could escape.

Escape? This time, it was my own voice shouting. My arm and ankle burned, but I didn't care about either one. I had to stop Josh from getting away. The VW was only a few feet off when I stepped into its path, waving my hands to attract attention. Behind the arc described on the shimmering glass by the wipers, I saw Josh instinctively wrench the steering wheel to one side.

A voice roared in my ear. Someone grabbed my arm and yanked it hard; it was the one with the bullet in it, and my knees buckled from the agony. There was a scream, a confused smashing noise.

I fell to the grass, rolled over, was hit by a tidal wave of water. My head was knocked back to the earth. Then the pressure eased and I gulped a deep breath into my lungs.

Struggling to my feet, I found myself staring point-blank into the disgusted face of Joe Cass. He grabbed my arm again.

"Lay off," I yelped. "There's a bullet in it! Never mind me—get Mackenzie!"

"Don't worry about *him*," Cass yelled, pointing at the

swimming pool, "he's not going anywhere." The VW was in the water, bobbing slowly from side to side and emitting a thick spew of sludge. As I watched, it foundered and, with a coarse bubbling noise, began to settle to the bottom. A patrolman jumped into the water and began to swing a club against one of the side windows of the bus. It was like a slow-motion film. There was a sluggish impact, followed by the graceful splay of glass as the blow did its work. . . .

"I hope the bastard can swim!" Cass growled. "One more Boulder Clan death, and I *quit!*"

26

One of the cops took Josh to his room to change into dry clothes. Cass did the same for me. I stripped off my shirt and he examined the wound in my arm.

"Nothing serious," the deputy said, "but you'd better have it looked at before it becomes infected."

"If you'd staked out the Opry like I told you," I complained, "none of this would've happened."

"How the hell did I know the murderer was going to pull a stunt like that?" Cass grumbled. "Hilary and I talked it over, but neither of us figured on *that* kind of scene. I had one of my men there, and that would've been enough, considering—if *you* hadn't decided to start playing cops and robbers!"

"Thanks a lot, Joe!" I snapped. "Some thanks I get for chasing your killer all the hell over Nashville for the last half-hour!"

"*My* killer?" he sneered. "I've got *my* killer."

"What the hell are you talking about??"

"Hilary tipped me off to the murderer's identity—and

it's *not* Josh. All you did was turn him into one scared rabbit."

I sat on the edge of the bed, feeling dizzy. I thought it over and realized that I'd never seen the face of the person who'd pushed Dolly off the balcony. Forcing myself to think in spite of the insistent pain in my limbs, I reconstructed the chase through the Opry. I pictured the door to the dressing rooms in my mind and then remembered who was on the other side. . . .

"Samson!" I shouted, trying to rise. But Cass put a hand on my shoulder and gently shoved me back down.

"Relax," he told me, "it's not him, either."

"Who is it then?" I demanded. "And *where* is the killer?"

"On the critical list," Cass replied. "We had to rush her to Nashville General."

I stared at him blankly. Then, a few seconds later, it hit me and I started to laugh.

I didn't shut up till the doctor stuck a needle in my arm and the sedative knocked me out.

27

The pain in my arm woke me.

I was flat on my back in an unyielding bed.

Light flooded down mercilessly and I quickly shut my eyes, but in the brief glimpse I got, I saw a featureless white ceiling and part of an unadorned, institutional green wall.

"You should be glad he didn't put a bullet through your thick head," Hilary remarked with her characteristic charm. I tried to sit up, but a rush of dizziness came over me and I dropped back onto the pillow. "Are you all right?" she asked. I opened my eyes once more and saw Hilary standing near the bed. She wore a green tailored suit, and had her hand extended as if to touch my forehead. But she withdrew it with a jerk.

"What the hell did they give me?" I asked, voice husky.

"Nothing that'll do any permanent damage. Here." She poured a glass of water. "How's your arm?"

"It hurts," I answered, taking a drink. The vertigo slowly passed and I began to feel a little better. Looking around, I saw a small, featureless, hospital room containing a bed, porcelain nightstand, and a chair. "How do I rate a private room?" I asked. "Who's paying for it?"

"Who the hell do you think?" she countered. "It was the only way to keep the press from bugging you . . . or would you rather regale the *Banner* with the story of your idiotic chase?"

"Where's Dolly? How is she?" I asked.

She ignored the question. "Josh was already desperate; you almost sent him out of his skull, running after—"

"How's Dolly?" I demanded.

"I never saw anything so stupid!! As if you could make out a case—"

Cursing, I threw back the covers and tried to get out of bed. Hilary immediately pushed me back.

"Keep off that foot!" she ordered. "You already broke it once!"

"Then tell me about Dolly!"

"You *really* want to know?"

"Yes."

Pulling a chair over to the edge of the bed, she sat and regarded me curiously. "I'm beginning to think," Hilary mused, "that you're some kind of masochist, physical *and* emotional."

"Tell me about Dolly!" I prompted.

"Concussion. Multiple fractures of the skull and spine. Broken neck. She's unconscious, and they don't give her much chance of pulling through."

"My God." I pictured Dolly as I first saw her, hefting my luggage, refusing help. I tried to remember on which cheek the dimple appeared when she smiled.

"For God's sake, stop it!" Hilary spoke harshly. "She murdered two people."

"All right," I said, "let me have it point by point."

"Not now," she frowned.

"*Now!*" I was surprised at my own vehemence.

She again reached out her hand, but immediately withdrew it. "All right," she sighed, resignedly. "Lie back and I'll talk. . . ."

I was wrong on nearly every point. The pilocarpine was not administered in a cut: Amanda had swallowed a massive dose and though, according to the M. E., it has never been medically determined how much it takes to finish someone off, Dolly evidently poured in an entire bottle of eye drops. That was plenty, especially considering that it was a 6 percent solution, the strongest on the market.

"Dolly said and did a lot of things that could be taken more than one way," Hilary began, "but I wasn't on the road with you, so I could only evaluate her behavior second hand, and you were obviously prejudiced in her favor. Furthermore, the Boulder Clan has been together for years. You were an outsider trying to get a glimpse into a closed society. There were secrets, buried relationships you couldn't hope to fathom in such a short time. . . ."

"I was afraid you were prejudiced against Dolly," I said.

"Why?" Hilary asked coldly.

"Never mind," I said quickly. "Go on."

"For a while," she continued after a moment, "I suspected Pearl, since she was Josh's bedmate and stood to gain the lead spot in the act if Amanda dropped out of the picture. But after her body was discovered in the dressing room, everything began to fall into place. I did have two brainstorms, but most of the subsequent work was just a matter of talking with Joe Cass, setting him onto a few lines of investigation. That, and a certain amount of hindsight—"

"Okay," I interrupted, "you didn't get it all one-two-three. Never mind—just lay it all out neatly now, all right?"

"Don't be impatient," she said. "Motive is the most important consideration. At first, I thought Amanda's murder was either the result of a love triangle or else a case of professional jealousy. It turned out to be both."

"Dolly *did* want to be a solo singer," I admitted.

"You bet she did. Practically the first thing out of her mouth when she met you was how she never got to sing in the family act. She was preoccupied with the subject. On top of that, she told you right away about her early rivalry with Amanda, whom she'd resented for years. As for Pearl, it was clear the first time I saw the two sisters at Lisle's that they didn't get along at all. It was always Pearl who filled in for Amanda—not Dolly—even though she'd been in the act years before her younger sister. Furthermore, you already mentioned how Dolly was jealous of Pearl's vocal training."

I nodded. "So after Pearl got the solo spot on the telecast—"

"Don't jump ahead," Hilary warned. "The second point under 'motive' is the fact that Dolly obviously still wanted Josh."

"Obviously," I sneered, "only I don't believe it!"

"Gene, what the hell does it take to get through to you?!" Hilary snapped. "Why do *you* think Dolly was forced into murdering Pearl? When Josh cut her down like that at Charlie Lisle's, he was stepping all over Dolly just to show what a big man he was to Pearl whom he'd already pushed into the solo spot on the telecast. Do you remember the expression on Dolly's face that night? It was pitiful how much she still loved Josh and it showed."

"Then how come she spent so much time in my company?"

Hilary laughed mirthlessly. "First thing, she asks the new PR man for a date to hear her sing, but when she thinks she might get Josh alone, she breaks the date, then picks it up again when Josh doesn't buy what she's selling. Next, when Amanda was announced as soloist on the telecast, Dolly took it so hard she walked right past you in Lisle's office—"

I tried to protest, but there was no stopping her.

"At the governor's party, Dolly was so stunned by the news of the engagement she ran out afterward, totally ignoring you. During the day, of course, she could use a chauffeur and she also knew how to turn on the charm when she needed a witness for her macabre charade in the cemetery. That was when she got scared she'd be linked to Pearl's death, so she decided she'd better pretend to be a victim, too. But do you remember when you went to get her at the hospital? She wasn't too eager to greet you, then, was she?"

"She was embarrassed!" I argued.

"Then how come she ran right up to Josh afterward and kissed him?"

I said nothing.

"You were nothing but a convenience for Dolly," Hilary said scornfully. "Josh is her only man, and he's an obsession with her. I talked to him a while ago, before you woke up, and he finally told me all about their relationship. She was possessive beyond belief. What was Brian's phrase? 'She made him punch a time clock.' Ever since he walked out on her, she's been trying to get him back and has been hounding him unmercifully. Why do you think you seldom saw him on the road? Because Dolly was always with you, that's why; Josh was trying to avoid her.

"Another thing," Hilary said, taking a deep breath. "What Josh said was true about Dolly signing his name on checks *she* wrote. . . ."

Hilary paused, waiting for me to comment. I nodded, saying, "Then I suppose Dolly wrote both of the notes she showed to me."

"Of course she did. That's why the police didn't see any messages shoved under her door. Later, she wouldn't let you show the first note to the police for fear they'd compare it with Josh's handwriting and learn it was a forgery."

Rising, Hilary began to pace the narrow room. I shifted, propping myself on an elbow so I could watch her.

"There was one especially odd thing—the vastly different nature of the two murders. Amanda's death was an 'impossible' crime. It obviously had to be subtly plotted well ahead of time. Pearl's shooting, on the other hand, appeared to be brutal and hasty.

"What must have happened is that Dolly decided to kill Pearl that night at Lisle's, only a few hours before she actually did. Josh was being true to form, preening Pearl as new star of the act. Anyone who really knew him figured he planned to hitch his own career to Pearl's, just as he'd done with Amanda. After one murder, Dolly wasn't about to sit back and let Pearl reap the rewards."

"Wait a minute," I said. "On the way back from Lisle's, Dolly learned we were being tailed, and she must have figured it was the police."

Hilary nodded. "Which shows how resourceful she was. She picked the one place to go where no one would suspect her—the police station! Remember the sequence? We took her to the motel because she was 'worried about the press' and she put on dark glasses *so she wouldn't be recognized.*

While she was up in her room, Dolly must have phoned Pearl—"

"She didn't know where to reach her," I objected.

"Not for sure. But she did know where Josh liked to go drinking, so she made a few blind calls until she tracked down Pearl and lured her to the Opry, warning her not to tell Josh who was on the other end."

"How could she be sure Pearl wouldn't blab, anyway?"

Hilary shrugged. "I don't know for a fact. But if I were Dolly, I would have suggested that Josh poisoned Amanda, and that I had evidence, but needed Pearl's advice before doing anything about it."

"Okay," I agreed, "but *how* did Dolly kill Pearl while she was being questioned at the police station?"

"Correction," Hilary replied, still pacing. "She was not at the station house all that time. Joe Cass compared the times with me. When we left Dolly, she was going to the ladies' room. That was about ten o'clock. Now, Dolly didn't appear in Cass's office to give her statement *until* 10:27 P.M. What was she doing in the interval?"

I shrugged.

"This is the way it had to work: She ducked into the john, changed into another outfit—remember the big bag she brought with her?—scooted out a side door, ran to the Opry, killed Pearl and returned the same way."

"Where did she get Josh's gun?"

"He kept it in his dressing room. I asked, and Josh was sure Dolly knew it. After she used the gun, she left it with the body—"

"Wait! That's too much! *You* said she loved Josh—why would she frame him?"

"For that matter," Hilary countered, "why would she forge a note in his handwriting, show it to you, then fake a poisoning and destroy *both* the message and the incriminating liquor bottle?"

"Well?" I asked. "Why?"

"Because, brightness," she answered, exasperated, "she knew that any minute Josh would check to see what was taking Pearl so long at the Opry. He did, and as soon as he saw his gun, he panicked and took it back with him to the Ramada. Now, the next morning, the first news Josh received was that Dolly was almost 'killed' the night before at the cemetery. He heard how she smashed the flask with poison in it, and he grew suspicious. Sure enough, his hip flask was missing. . . ."

I spread my hands wide. "I still don't get what you're driving at. Why would Dolly only want Josh to think he was being 'set up'?"

"Jesus!" she said sourly, "I thought you broke your ankle, not your brain! Look, if Dolly didn't want to actually pin the murders on Josh, then the only thing she could have had in mind was coercion."

"Coercion? To do *what?*"

"To return to her; to marry Dolly again."

I frowned skeptically. "I find *that* hard to buy, Hilary, no matter—"

"My God!" She slapped a hand against her forehead. "You *are* hung up on her! Gene, can't you *see* how sick Dolly is? That gargoyle scene in the cemetery—that alone ought to convince you. If Dolly weren't in the country-music field, she probably would have been rehearsing Wagner's love-death."

"Meaning?"

"I'll translate," Hilary said. "Why do you think Dolly picked the Ann Rawlings Sanders monument? Because she identified with a girl who killed herself for love. She was already considering what she'd do if Josh turned her down—in spite of everything she'd tried."

That made me think of Dolly and Josh in the balcony.

"All right," said Hilary, "let's go to the time right after the awards ceremony. It was Dolly who informed the press she and Josh were going on the road together—not Josh. Later that night, Josh says he told her he'd do no such thing. The next day, Dolly begged Josh to meet her in the balcony. By then, Josh was pretty suspicious of her but he decided that if she was planning something, he'd tell her he'd rather go to jail on a framed rap than marry her a second time."

"He never would have had the guts."

"Of course not. But he figured if Dolly *was* planning to frame him, he could always run for the border. But he never thought she'd jump off the balcony. . . ."

"Neither did you," I murmured.

"Please don't remind me," Hilary shuddered. "Until then, I didn't know just how sick she was."

"But maybe her fall was an accident?"

Hilary shook her head. "Then why did she write a second note and show it to you, giving you a chance to compare the handwriting? No, she was bent on framing Josh, unless he married her. Then, at least, I suppose, they'd both become tragic lovers, the kind that country ballads are sometimes written about."

A new thought occurred to me then. I didn't like it. "Why," I asked Hilary, "didn't you tell me any of your suspicions? I thought we agreed to tackle Amanda's murder together."

Hilary admitted that was so, but pointed out that my infatuation with Dolly made it impossible to confide in me. "I wanted to tell you what was on my mind, but you remember the fight we got into when I tried. I wondered, too, whether I could trust you to keep your mouth shut: if you repeated something to Dolly—"

"That," I stated vehemently, "is a gross insult! You ought to know me better!"

"Really?" Hilary replied sweetly. "What should I call this touching display? An example of company loyalty?"

"Yes—you bitch!"

"Don't call me that!"

"Then don't act like one."

"If you weren't already an invalid," Hilary snapped, "I might make you one."

"That's what you think!" I yelled. "The next time you try to use a knee on me, I'll wrap—"

Just then, Joe Cass walked in. "Pipe down, you two," he growled, "they can hear you halfway to the elevators." We shut up.

After inquiring how I felt, Cass turned to Hilary. "You had it pretty well figured," he said. "We found those sunglasses in Dolly's bag: They *were* prescription lenses. The ophthalmologist was all the way over in Smith Center, Kansas, but we traced him from the case. Dolly went to him while she was on the road several months ago. He diagnosed glaucoma, fitted her with special glasses, and prescribed Pilocar, a brand of pilocarpine hydrochloride eye drops."

Hilary nodded, self-satisfied. But I was still feeling argumentative. "Hold on. You can't tell me that you deduced that Dolly had eye trouble. Except for those sunglasses, she never—" I stopped. Memories suddenly began to crowd in on me.

"Uh–huh," said Hilary. "Remember all the headaches she complained about, the tense lines around her eyes? She *needed* to wear glasses, but didn't. Ever since the doctor warned her about the toxicity of the eye drops, Dolly must have thought about using them on Amanda, but she could only do so if nobody knew she had access to them. Dosing herself in private was no problem—but the glasses were another matter."

Cass concurred. "Pilocarpine poisoning is so uncommon that Dolly couldn't take a chance being even remotely connected with eye trouble, let alone glaucoma. I wonder whether she was planning to develop her affliction a long time after the murder? Even that would have been risky."

"All right," I sighed, "you've convinced me anew of your mental luster. Go ahead and show off, Hilary, tell me how Dolly actually poisoned Amanda. I don't suppose any of the drug was finally traced to the water?"

Cass shook his head.

Hilary spoke. "I had one question to unravel right from the first: Why did Amanda sing 'I'll Never Call You Sweetheart Again' at the governor's party? She swore to Charlie Lisle that she'd never perform it in public. Why the change of heart? For that matter, why was she so opposed to singing it in the first place? She wrote it herself.

"I got the answers to those questions from members of the Clan, along with information I gleaned from the press clips. But I still didn't know how the poison was administered, and I didn't catch on until *you* said something shortly after Pearl's body was found."

"Me?" I asked.

"Yes; you used the phrase 'magic tricks.' That got me thinking about the principle of misdirection. Magicians employ it as their chief method of psychological deception. If a conjurer holds one hand loosely by his side and stretches the other in the air, pointing to the outstretched fist, you can be sure the hand doing the work is the one you're *not* watching—the one at his side.

"So," Hilary continued, "if we apply this idea to the poisoning, what do we come up with? Gene, you watched Amanda drink water from a glass on the podium, then you saw her have a violent seizure. But suppose that reaction was really a form of misdirection. What then?"

She looked at me expectantly, waiting. When I got it, it made me wince. "Everybody ate lunch together," I groaned, "so the only other time Amanda could have been poisoned was *after* she drank from the pitcher."

"Right," Hilary said. "It *was*, however, imperative that Amanda be thirsty enough to drink, so Dolly suggested lunch at a Mexican restaurant where spicy food would be served. Later, she was at the side of the stage, waiting for Amanda to keel over. She told you which dressing room to carry her sister to—and then what did she do?"

"And then," I said slowly, "Dolly sent me out of the room to fetch the rest of the Clan."

"That's it," Cass agreed. "That's the only time Dolly could have given Amanda a swig of poisoned booze. How do you like her style? Nobody thought of looking for the fatal hip flask after Dolly hid it in the dressing room because no one even suspected it existed! Everyone was positive the poison was in the drinking water, so Dolly had plenty of time later to sneak the actual container out of the Opry."

Shaking my head, I marveled at Dolly's brazenness. She could have gotten rid of the flask in private, instead of smashing it in my sight, but the very action of destroying it served to convince me that someone else was guilty.

"Do you think there was any poison left in the flask when Dolly drank?" I asked Hilary.

She shrugged. "Who knows? I told you she was sick . . .

she *might* have gone to that extent just to be more convinc-
ing, although I don't think she would have taken such a risk
—not when she still thought she had a chance of holding
Josh."

"Well, you could ask her about it," Cass remarked.

"Who?" I demanded, "What do you mean?"

"Dolly regained consciousness," the deputy said. "She
asked for you."

I started to get out of bed, but Cass put a hand on my
shoulder. "Slow down, junior. I'll get you a wheelchair."
He telephoned the desk for one, but was told there'd be a
delay of several minutes.

I was impatient. "Did Dolly say anything else?" I asked.
"How coherent is she?"

"Enough," said Cass. "They didn't want to let me in to
see her, but they couldn't keep me out. I told her we had
evidence, and she was too weak to argue about it. She only
wanted to know whether she could see Josh."

"And—?"

"And Josh wasn't interested. She asked for you next."

Hilary was fidgeting. I asked her what was wrong.

"Before you got sidetracked," she said, "I *was* going to
finish explaining how Dolly poisoned Amanda."

At that point, I didn't really care, but I told her to go
ahead and dazzle me with her ratiocinative prowess. She
ignored the sarcasm.

"The question," said Hilary, "is what Dolly put in the water to cause Amanda to react so violently?"

I remarked, "You didn't see how fierce a response it was,
either, but I did, and I can tell you it was no mere bad taste
that Amanda noticed."

"Precisely," Hilary replied, "but even after I figured out
how Dolly had misdirected everyone, I couldn't manage

the answer to the water trick. Then I heard Dolly sing her sister's song—and I suddenly realized how it was done."

"About that song," I said. "You didn't explain why Amanda decided to sing it at the governor's party. . . ."

"I'm just coming to that. Remember that she changed the lyrics that night? Josh already had Amanda believing her late husband, Merrill Gannett, once slept with Dolly. Marrying Josh was the best way Amanda could see to get even with her sister, because she knew how much Dolly still wanted him. So when Amanda sang, *'But I'll find another love to ease the stinging,'* she was taunting Dolly just before springing the news of the engagement on her.

"But the alteration surprised other people, too—the audience. Why? Because everyone knew how significant that song was to Amanda! Writing it had to be torture, and once she'd recorded it, she didn't think she could ever bear to perform it again. *Why?*"

"You're telling it," I said.

"Think how Amanda reacted to her husband's death. Because she'd arranged a picnic where her husband suffered a fatal allergic reaction, she thought Merrill Gannett's death was her fault. Her family had to put Amanda in a rest home for six months because she tried to commit suicide. If she was *that* far gone, what saved her from spending the rest of her life at the funny farm?"

I nodded. "Sublimation."

"That's it on the button," Cass remarked. "If you've heard enough country music, and if you meet some of the people who write it—as I have—you learn they put their own personal sorrows and worries right into their music. Amanda wrote 'I'll Never Call You Sweetheart Again' because, for her, creating a song was the only way she knew to overcome the grief and guilt she felt at her husband's death.

How does the line go? '*Well, I cry each time I dream I hear you singing.*' Hell, she had to mean that literally!"

"And the next line," said Hilary, "is similar—'*Though the pain I feel is nothing like your pain.*' That—"

"Never mind," I said, repressing a shudder, "don't say anything else, I've figured it out."

It was horrible. The bitter, self-inflicting pun: "*I'll never call you sweetheart again.*" The literal reference in the next-to-last line: "*Yet no other love will come to ease the stinging. . . .*"

Merrill Gannett suffered a fatal allergic reaction after stepping on an insect. Now I knew it must have been a bee. And poor tormented Amanda, who couldn't even hear the word "picnic" mentioned without growing hysterical. . . .

There was only one substance Dolly could have smeared on the glass to produce the convulsive nausea I observed.

It was named in the second verse of Amanda's song.

28

Cass took me to Dolly's room and promised to wait outside while I talked with her. Samson and Brian were in the hall, waiting. When he saw me, the big man waved and glumly asked how I was doing. A little way off, Charlie Lisle was talking with Josh; they both avoided me.

Samson held the door open and I wheeled into the room, a cheerless cell similar to the one I'd just quitted. The nurse announced me, told me I could only stay a few minutes, then left me alone with Dolly.

Her head was covered with bandages, and she was in some kind of harness. She lay on her back, staring at the ceiling with a vague, faraway expression in her eyes; I recognized the wistful look I'd first seen in her photograph.

"Gene?" she asked, her voice aspirate, barely a whisper, "where are you? I can't see you."

I explained I was in a wheelchair, then moved closer. Grabbing the nightstand, I managed to stand on my uninjured leg by supporting my weight with one hand on the tabletop.

"What happened to you?" Dolly whispered. I told her,

and she sighed ruefully, "I guess it's gonna be a long while before either of us does any more prancing."

I wasn't going for any small talk.

"You murdered Amanda, didn't you?"

Dolly's mouth silently formed the word, yes; she was unable to incline her head.

"Gene," she entreated, "*don't* hate me—Amanda deserved to die! She was drunk the night she smashed up the car and killed my pappy." Her eyes misted over. "None of this would have happened if Pappy'd lived a couple more years. He eventually would've let me sing a solo in the act, wouldn't he?"

"How about Pearl?" I demanded. "Did she deserve to die, too?"

Her mood instantly changed. Features contorting with rage, Dolly's voice became a harsh rasp. "Pearl was *trash!*" she spat, "I wasn't gonna let her latch onto Josh like *that. . . .*"

I shook my head. "God almighty," I said, "you *are* one hell of an actress."

Another lightning metamorphosis occurred. "Gene," she said earnestly, "I don't understand. Please don't—"

"*Cut it,*" I ordered. "You manipulated me like a goddamned puppet, but you're not getting away with it anymore. What was that scene in the cemetery—a dress rehearsal for the big leap? How about the way you wept over Amanda? Why did you even go along with her to the hospital in the first place? Just to study the way she died so you could reproduce the symptoms when *you* pretended to be poisoned?" I dropped into the wheelchair and pushed myself toward the door. "I've had enough of you, Dolly, for one lifetime."

"*Please* don't go, Gene!" She sounded desperate.

"All right," I said, not moving. "Stop the phony crying and I'll stay."

"It *isn't* phony," Dolly protested, tearfully. "But I'm *trying* to stop." I wheeled back to the bed. She attempted a smile, but it was a miserable failure. "I *know* I can't expect you to believe me," Dolly whispered hoarsely, "but I really *was* upset over Amanda's death. If I'd ever known how awful the effects were, I'd never have used my medicine. I'm telling the truth, Gene!"

"All right, Dolly, it's true. So what?"

"That's why I shot Pearl," she explained. "Compared with that poison, a bullet was more merciful—"

"More merciful!" I exclaimed. "Jesus, Dolly, you can't be *that* sick—can you?"

She stared at me, horrified.

Neither of us spoke for a long time.

The nurse looked in. When she saw Dolly's face, she tried to shoo me out, but Dolly pleaded for a few more minutes alone with me, and the nurse begrudgingly complied—but not before she'd shot a look in my direction that would have withered a cactus.

After she left, Dolly asked me why Josh hadn't come to see her yet.

So that's it, I thought.

"I don't know," I said, carefully controlling myself. "Would you like me to bring him here for you?"

Dolly's eyes shone. "Would you do that for me, Gene?"

"*No, damn you!*" It was like slapping her face. "What the hell do you think I am?" I demanded bitterly. "You've used me all along, pretending you cared about me. Now you think all you have to do is cry and faithful Gene will drag that bastard in here to say hello. *Forget it.*"

I would have said more, but the look in her eyes stopped

me. I'd seen it once before, and I had no defense against it. It was the same expression I'd seen on her face Sunday morning when she rushed into my arms to apologize for the way she'd behaved at the post-awards party.

"No matter what Hilary probably told you," Dolly said softly, "and no matter what you think of me now, Gene, I *do* love you."

"Uh–huh," I said sarcastically, "and of course you couldn't care less about Josh."

"No," she replied. "I love Josh, too."

I turned away from her. "Very pretty, Dolly. Only I don't buy it."

"It's true, nevertheless. I know I deserved everything you said, I *did* use you at first—it's true. But somewhere along the line, I started to care, in spite of myself."

"Stop lying!" I demanded angrily.

"Please turn around," Dolly pleaded, "I have to tell you something. *Please*, Gene, look at me!"

Reluctantly, I faced her and she said something, but it was so soft I couldn't hear. I bent over and Dolly whispered in my ear.

"If I'd *only* been using you," she said, "there would have been no reason for me to become your lover, Gene. . . ."

Our eyes met. *You bitch*, I thought, *you're still lying to me . . . I know you are. . . .*

But I kissed her just the same.

Later on, Josh dropped by to see how Dolly was feeling. If he hadn't, I would have broken his arm.

POSTSCRIPT

She died that night of a blood clot on the brain, a result of her head injuries. The family tried to keep the funeral private, but there were still plenty of red-necks gawking, not to mention the reporters. Samson asked me to be one of the pallbearers, so I had to fight off a few journalists, too.

At the cemetery, the rain had turned the earth to brown ooze, and as we slogged across the grass, the mud streaked our shoes and cuffs. I'd been given a pair of gray gloves to wear; they were tight and clammy and clung to the flesh.

After a terse, controlled show, the funeral director told us to put the gloves on the coffin top. I pulled them with difficulty from my fingers, tossed them onto the box and saw one glove skitter along the surface, find the empty space between the supportive planks and plunge beneath.

I hoped some meticulous functionary wouldn't later try to retrieve this unexpected final cushion for Dolly's head.

I hadn't set foot in the Thunderbird since I'd chased Josh, so Brian borrowed the Lincoln and drove us to the airport in time to catch the 2:15 for LaGuardia. Hilary insisted on buying the drinks, and I didn't argue. Considering the air fare it was costing her, and the fact that we were leaving Nashville without a client, she was in a reasonably decent mood. But we didn't have too much to say to each other during the flight.

A couple of days later, an official-looking envelope from Charlie Lisle arrived in the mail. He wanted us to stand the cost of replacing the VW bus. Hilary got on the phone immediately and explained the situation to Willie Frost, our attorney. He straightened Lisle out quickly. After hearing about damages for the slug Josh put in my arm, the manager decided it was better to call the situation a standoff.

Naturally, the Boulder Clan was no longer in existence as an act. Samson announced his retirement soon afterward and went into partnership in a music-publishing business with Lisle; the first song in their catalog was Amanda's. Josh continued to perform solo, but he didn't do too well on the circuit: Too many details of his relations with the Boulder women came out in the press, and the bookers let Josh know his behavior wasn't popular with Middle America.

The real surprise was Brian—he let his hair grow, affected shades, lost his paunch, and started an acid-rock group. The last I heard he was cutting an album for a medium-sized label, and "Cash Box" was betting on him.

After we returned from Music City, I got several calls from Marty Gold. He was still checking for details on camotillo. To this day, he hasn't found any.

Several weeks later, I was opening the mail when I discovered a small package addressed to Hilary from Harriet Marker of the Thomas Agency; she was the woman who'd recommended us to the Boulder Clan in the first place. I left it on Hilary's desk, but when she came into the office later on and found it, she brought it right back to me.

"It's yours," she said, avoiding my eyes and walking quickly out of the room.

I opened the package. Inside was a seven-inch LP phonograph record, privately cut. An enclosed note from Harriet Marker apologized to Hilary for not being able to obtain the disc from the master tapes sooner. I took it to the phonograph and put it on.

> *I have seen your eyes and know that they are yearning,*
> *I have fled them down the years, but all in vain . . .*

A cold chill ran down my spine. It was Dolly's voice.

> *And the sorrow in my heart is always burning*
> *For I'll never call you sweetheart again.*

The record was a transcription of her appearance on the NBC country-music awards telecast. I listened to it all the way through, then stood there while the needle scratched against the inner groove.

When Hilary reentered the office a few moments later, I was standing in the same position.

"Did I make a mistake," she asked softly, "sending for the record?"

I shook my head, not trusting myself to speak.

Walking to the phonograph, Hilary picked up the tone arm and told me to listen again to the last verse. She replaced the stylus on the disc.

> *Well, I cry each time I dream I hear you singing,*
> *Though the pain I feel is nothing like your pain.*
> *But I'll find another love to ease the stinging*
> *And I'll never call you sweetheart again.*

"Did you hear it?" she asked, turning off the machine.

I nodded. "She sang Amanda's revised line."

"Yes," Hilary Quayle said quietly. "I thought you'd want to know. . . ."